William Theodore Parkes

The spook ballads

William Theodore Parkes

The spook ballads

ISBN/EAN: 9783743309227

Manufactured in Europe, USA, Canada, Australia, Japa

Cover: Foto ©Andreas Hilbeck / pixelio.de

Manufactured and distributed by brebook publishing software
(www.brebook.com)

William Theodore Parkes

The spook ballads

SPOOK BALLADS

BY

W. THEODORE PARKES.

Crown 8vo, Cloth gilt, 5s.

POPULAR EDITION 2s.

———

LONDON :

SIMPKIN, MARSHALL, HAMILTON, KENT, & CO., LIMITED.

And all Booksellers.

CHEERS OF THE PRESS!

"Ingoldsby, Thomas Hood, W. S. Gilbert,—these are the names that occur to one in trying to 'place' Mr. Parkes after reading this volume of rollicking, verbal and pictorial fun. THE SPOOK BALLADS are in no sense imitations of any of those classics of the comic muse, yet we find in them the same thorough abandonment to 'the humour of the thing.'"—*The Publisher's Circular*

"A substantial volume introducing a Comic Poet, who in the future may give us a modern Ingoldsby. Mr. Parkes has an intellectual touch to his drollery and his sense of the possible humours of versification is pleasantly keen, the SPOOK BALLADS is far above the contemporary average of the lighter rhymesters. Mr. Parkes wields a sprightly pencil, and he has illustrated his verses lavishly and with effect."—*The Stage.*

"Not only are the literary merit of these fantastic ballads of a high order, but the illustrations by the author are of such a humorous nature as to give a unique pleasure to the reader."—*The Morning Leader.*

"Well written, well illustrated, and funny is a combination of good qualities not often met with even in the Spook world, so Messrs. Simpkin, Marshall, Hamilton, Kent, and Co., ought to be well pleased with their publication."—*The Illustrated Sporting and Dramatic News.*

"Dealing largely with ghosts and legends embracing a dash of diablerie such as would have been dear to the heart of Ingoldsby. There is a rugged force in 'The Girl of Castlebar' that will always make it tell in recitation ; and even greater success in this direction has attended 'The Fairy Queen,' a story unveiling the seamy side, with quaint humour and stern realism. It is specially worthy of note that Mr. Parkes's skill in versification has received the warmest acknowledgment from those best qualified to appreciate the bright local coloring as well as the blending of fancy and fun."—*Lloyd's Weekly Newspaper.*

" A cheery and spirited production, and full of fun ; the style reminds one of 'Bon Gaultier,' the style and illustrations combined inevitably recall the famous 'Bab Ballads.' Indeed it is hard to say which is the most felicitous, the draughtsman or the poet."—*The Bookseller*.

" In the attractive SPOOK BALLADS, the talented Irish artist has displayed qualities to a remarkable degree. There are many pieces reciters will be glad to lay hold of, while the Ballads and Illustrations are full of the pleasing humour which characterises all Mr. Parkes' work, and which will serve to cheer and to amuse many readers."—*The Sun*.

" As the combined production of a clever pencil and a clever pen, this volume may be said to be unique. These poems are pure fun of the most entirely frolicsome kind, hung upon the peg of a quaint idea. ' The German Band ' rises to a really tragic pathos. The illustrations are either quaint, droll, or dainty, or partake of broad caricature."—*The Citizen*.

" It contains a store of humour that will delight and amuse the reader, who will be sure to re-read the many capital lays. Just the thing for reciters. The Artist, his own Illustrator, shines here as conspicuously as in the kindred branch of Authorship."—*British and Colonial Printer and Stationer*.

" Mr. Parkes is clever and polished alike in the expression of humour and pathos. Indescribably funny is his story of the deluge as told by 'Antediluvian Pat O'Toole,' and a note of grim tragedy is struck in the tale of 'John McKune.' Rollicking lays, many of them admirably adapted for recitation, go to make a delightful book, which has the uncommon merit of being well illustrated by Mr. Parkes, who is as skilful an artist as he is an author." *Photographic Journal*.

" SPOOK BALLADS possess an amount of boisterous humour and variety of quaint versification which make them excellent and refreshing reading. The book owes a good deal of its charm to the author's clever and laughable illustrations which are plentifully besprinkled in its pages."—*The Weekly Sun*

" There is a good store of pleasant humour in SPOOK BALLADS, by Theodore Parkes, who also has a happy gift with the pencil, as witness the illustrations, the fare he provides certainly deserves a really grateful 'grace after meat.' " *The People*.

" In his attractive volume, THE SPOOK BALLADS, Mr. Theodore Parkes has shown himself to be not only an author but an artist of considerable talents." *Weekly Budget*

" The fun is good humoured and light-hearted, and better than most popular verse as to rhyme and metre. The illustrations are really clever and range from broad farce to charming little head and tail pieces that are graceful and suggestive."—*Borderland*.

" Ballads all of which are undeniably clever. A book which will be gratefully turned to by all who seek occasional relaxation in the best of good company." *The Surveyor*.

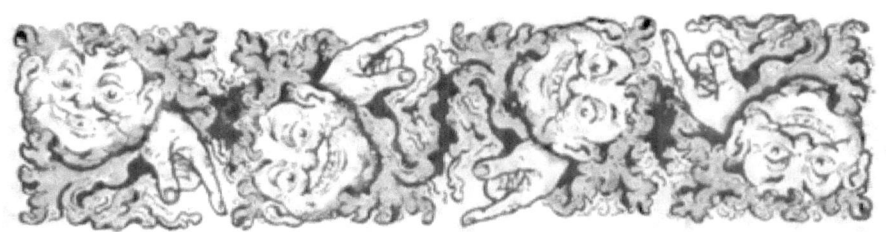

THE SPOOK BALLADS.

THE
SPOOK BALLADS

BY

WM. THEODORE PARKES

Author of "THE BARNEY BRADEY BROCHURES"

———

ILLUSTRATED BY THE AUTHOR

———

LONDON :
SIMPKIN, MARSHALL, HAMILTON, KENT & Co., LIMITED.
1895

CONTENTS.

Bohemians, hail!

The daylight dreams of many a time,
    When song, and rhythmic story,
Were tuned, and voiced for Bigot, and in gay Bohemian
        ears,
Bring welcome wraiths of joyous nights, thro' whirling clouds
        of glory ;
    The incense of the social weed, o'er spirit cup that cheers.
With hail ! to Cycle speedmen, and the boaters of Dunleary,
    Clontarf, and the Harmonic, where we sang with
        midnight chimes,
The smokers of Conservatives, and Liberal Unions cheery,
    I weave regretful tribute to their jovial social times ;
For autumn gales of life have blown those festal hours
        asunder,
    And scattered far by land and sea, the steps of many a
        one,
And some alas ! beneath the sod, for evermore gone under,
    Have left a rainbow thro' the mist of grief that they
        have won,

But slantha! to the hearts, and hands, of those who yet
        remaining,
    Do carry down traditions of that bright Bohemian
        throng,
And slantha! to the soulful sheen, of life-light never waning
    From Old Eblana's heaven of her social art, and song.

And here's to all Bohemians, of whatever rank, or station,
    Whatever tint, or black or tan, or creed you are by
        birth,
Sweet voices of the earth's romance, of every land, or nation,
    Hail! brothers, in the carnival of music, song, and
        mirth:
So fill we tankards, or the glass, for draught with lusty
        cheering,
    Of honor to a crowning toast, with greeting heart and
        hand,
As everlasting goal, for letters, art, and song, and beering,
    Hip, hip, hurrah! vive! hoc! and skoal! to Fleet
        Street and the Strand!

THE GHOST OF HAMPTON COURT

THE following verses, a remarkable supernatural interview is narrated. It is now for the first time launched into publicity, on the authority, and with the approbation of a quaint old friend of mine, Professor Simon Chuffkrust, a savant who has daringly groped his way through certain gloomy mysteries of occult science.

The confidential and impressive manner of Chuffkrust, is jewelled with eyes of sparkling jet, semitoned behind a screen of moonblue spectacles.

His voice is of such convincing suasion, that it is a novel and interesting experience to hear him relate with circumstantial enthusiasm, the ghostly interview afforded him by a fortuitous chance within the interesting grounds of Hampton Court. His is a testimony most reliable, and calculated to establish as a fact the actual presence of supernatural shadows in that historic locality.

It also hints at the necessity, and use, of making the ghost a more familiar study, whereby the belated world would rid itself of much unnecessary fright, consequent on the invariable habit of spasmodically avoiding the familiar advances of the common or bedroom spook.

IN Hampton Court I wandered on a twilight evening grey,
    Amidst its mazy precincts I had lost my tourist way,
And while I cogitated, on a seat of carven stone,
I heard beneath an orange tree, an elongated groan !
I crinkled with astonishment, 'twas not a fit of fright,
For loud elastic wailings, I have heard at twelve at night,
The midnight peace disturbing in the lamplit streets below,
But this was uttered in an unfamiliar groan of woe,
And Hampton Court I wot had got some questionable nooks,
In which it harboured spectres, and disreputable spooks,
In which it shrouded headless Queens, and shades of evil
    Kings
With ill-conditioned titled knaves, in lemans leading strings.

I listened ! 'twas a voice that cried as 'twere from out the dust
Of time, that clogged its music, with a husk of mould and
    rust,
A voice that once as tenor, might have won a slight repute,
But combination now of asthma, whooping cough, and flute.

I sauntered towards the orange tree, and lo ! the gloaming
    thro'
I saw a man in trunk and hose, and silver buckled shoe,
With ruffles and embroidered vest, in wig without a hat,
Inclining to the contour, which is designated fat.

Just then the waxing moonlight bloomed
            behind, and lifed the stain
Of color thro' him, like a Saint
                upon a window pane,
I could not spare such noted chance; so
            stepping from the gloom,
I bowed politely and exclaimed
                    "A Spectre I presume?"
With glad pathetic wondered look, but still in
            tones of woe,
He answered thus, "Alack! ah me I am exactly so"
And confidential gleam of hope across his features grew,
Which gave me courage thus to start a social interview.
"I pray of thee to speak, alas! why grims it so with thee?
Some evil canker nips thy peace, divulge thy wrongs to me,
That I may give thee hope, for I am one to sympathize
With manhood's lamentation, as with womanhood, her sighs,
But ha! Mayhap it fits your jest, with elongated groan,
To seek to fright me, as I'm here in Hampton Court alone,

To wreck my spirits
    as of old has
    been the game of
    spook,"

The spectre turned
    upon me with a
    sad reproachful
    look.
And cried, "Alack!
    that living men,
    so long have held
    it good,

To flee from Ghosts, and hence the Ghost is not yet understood,
Now as for me, I moan it not, for jest of idle sport,
My task, it is as murdered Ghost, to haunt in Hampton Court!
I play the victim to a spook, who chucked me down a stair,
Thro' being caught too near my lady's bedroom unaware."

" Poor shade of ill mischance!" I sobbed, the while a way-
        ward tear,
Tricked out along my nose, and lodged upon my tunic here,
" I pray that thou would'st tell me all, withholding ne'er a jot,
For I might do thee service, in some most unlikely spot,"

"O blessed chance!" the Ghost exclaimed, "Thou art the
        only one
Of all men else, who spoke me so, they always turn and run!
Thou art the first, that I have seen drop sympathetic tears,
Responsive to my moanings, aye for full one hundred years!
And so I feel that I can speak in unreserving tone,
And give thee cause for this alack! my chronic nightly groan!

When I was in my thirties, I engaged to mind the spoons,
Of Colonel Sir John Bouncer, of the Sixty-fifth Dragoons,
And tho' of lowly stature, I am proud I was by half,
More manly than the footman, by step, and chest, and calf.
With frontispiece well favored, in a frame of powdered wig,
I wot amongst the female sex, I joyed a game of tig,
I played the captivating spark, till Colonel Bouncer caught
Me jesting with my Mistress, and he spake with furious
        haught,

Expressed him his disfavor loud, unto my Lady thus,
"An' thou do not discharge the knave, 'twill cause some
    future fuss,
The cock-a-dandy bantam, pillory graduate, and scoff
On manhood, give him notice!" but no, she begged me off.

   ❊   ❊   ❊   ❊   ❊   ❊   ❊

It was not long thereafter, an early postman bore
A warrant for the Colonel, to start for Singapore,
He sailed, and in the August, 'twas just ten months away
He stayed, and he was due in town, upon the first of May,
'Twas on that ninth of August at twelve o'clock at night,
'Thro Bouncer Hall I wandered, to see that all was right;
And in my course of searching, to check the silver stock,
I chanced upon the key, with which my Lady wound the
    clock,
A Louis clock she valued, it was on the mantel shelf
In her boudoir, her habit was to wind it up herself,
I brought it to her bedroom, and scratched a single knock,
And asked her through the keyhole, if she had wound the
    clock.

My words were scarcely uttered,
    when from another door,
        I heard a foot,
that should have been that night
        in Singapore!
        I saw an eye,
that should have seen that night
        a foreign shore,
    "Ha! Caitiff knave!!"
        He shouted,
'Twas all I heard, no more,

He collared me by neck, and breech,

       and swept me off the floor,
   And bore me down the corridor,
And hoisting me as light as cork, an act I could not check,
He flung me down the oaken stair,

       and wanton cracked my neck !
For that he paid the penalty, one day on Tyburn tree,
Alack ! it was the sorest deed, the Law could wreak for me
For when it made a Ghost of him,

       he came, and sought me out,
Where haunting at my Lady's door,

       I heard the self-same shout,
        Of " Caitiff knave ! ! "

    The pity on't ! he took me unaware,

Once more by gripping of my
  breech, and tossed me down
  the stair !
Night after night he compas-
  sed it, nor recked he who
  was there
But by my crop, and grip of
  trunks, he bumped me
  down the stair !
Thus mortified by evil fate,
  his widow nightly wept,
To hear the periodic row, and
  scarce a wink she slept ;
She daily sought to lay his ghost
  by penance and by prayer,
And got a brace of saintly
  monks, to exorcise the scare

With holy water sprinked about, a jot he did not care!
But seized me with a fiercer grip, and jocked me down the
    stair!
And mocked the frightened monks, who flew, with fringe of
    standing hair.
At last his widow could not reck his evil conduct there,
                    She moved to otherwhere.
The only tenants that remained in Bouncer Hall, were rats,
Until 'twas taken down, to build some fashionable flats,
And when the workmen moved the stair, I wot he was cut up,
To see its broken banisters, upon a cart put up.

But vengeance of his hate for me, remained a danger yet,
To find a suitable resort, to work it out he set,
And tapped the telephone, until he heard of that resort ;
It is an antient oaken stair, that's here in Hampton Court,
'Twas vacant of a Ghost, I faith, a lobby to be let,
And with some Royal Spook, he had a ghostly compact set,
And then he brought me here to work,
  his midnight murder yet.
An hour ago, accosting me, says
  he to me, " Prepare !
Be ready ! for once more to-night,
  I'll crock thee down the stair '

To-night, a cousin German of the
  noble house of Teck

Will occupy the bedroom, and I'll
  have to crack thy neck !"

In yonder wing, and up the stairs as high as thou canst go,
There is the bedroom, with a door, of casement rather low,

And if thou stay a night therein, thy sleep might wake for
    shock,
Of scratching on the door, and keyhole cry, to wind your
    clock,
And then the shout of

                "Caitiff knave!"

                        And if thou'rt bold and dare,
To peer out on that lobby then, he crocks me down the stair!
And leaves thee shivering in thy shirt, with fright and
    besomed hair!
I've heard the County Council, for the City weal is rife,
I'd hold it as a favor, if thou'ds't intimate that life
Is perilled on that lobby, and suggest in thy report,
That lifts would be more suitable, than stairs in Hampton
    Court."

Then with a comprehensive
    wail of anguish at his fate,
He gradually vanished thro'
    the grating of a gate,
And left me sorely puzzled,
    in a sad reflective state,
Then up a creeping tree,
    and spout,
    with stern resolve of hate
Compressed within my
    breast for Bouncer's evil
        ghost I clomb,

        And slipping thro' the window frame with feline
    caution dumb,

I slid behind a folding screen, and with a craning neck,
I listened for the snoring of the Colonel Van der Teck,
> But not a soul had come that night into the room to rest,
> There was no cousin German, and the bed was yet
> unpressed ;
A knavish and mendacious trick it was of Bouncer's Ghost,
To crack his butler's neck again, but with some beans and toast,
> I picketed behind the door, on eager ear to catch,
> The slightest human murmur, thro' the keyhole of
> the latch,
At last it came ! the midnight yet, was booming from a clock,
When lo ! a scratching on the door, and half-way thro' the lock,
I heard the question, and with shout, I gave the ghosts a shock,
By springing to the lobby, like a chip of blasting rock !
And bounded twixt the spectres, with the rage of fighting cock,

Then facing Colonel Bouncer's Ghost,
> " Thou caitiff spook " I cried,
" Was it for this, that Shakespeare wrote, and Colonel
Hampden died ?

> For this! that Cromwell lopped a royal head as
> traitor knave?
> For this! that all his cuirassiers were sworn to pray
> and shave?

Was it for this we lost a world! when George the Third
was king?
For this! that laureates have lived of royal deeds to sing?

> For this! the printing press was made, torpedoes,
> dynamite?
> The iron ships, and bullet proof cuirass to scape the
> fight?

Was it for this! we've wove around the world a social net
Of speaking steel, that thou should'st perpetrate thy murder
yet?

> Out! out on thee! as traitor of thine oath unto
> the crown!
> By gripping of thy butler, by his breech to jock
> him down,

Was it for this! that justice wrung thy neck on Tyburn tree,
To expiate the direful debt to justice due by thee?

> For this! did Lord Macaulay write "The Lays of
> Antient Rome?"
> For this! did Government send out to bring us
> Jabez home?

Have we been privileged to pay our swollen rates and tax?
And legislative rights imposed upon the noble's backs?

> For this! was England parcelled out amongst the
> Norman few,
> That thou should'st haunt in Hampton Court thy
> noisome work to do?

For this! is London soaring up, to Babel flights of flats

As cross between a poorhouse, and a prison ?—are top hats
Still worn by busmen, beadles, undertakers, men of prayer!
That thou should'st cause the lieges to irradiate their hair,
With horror at thy felon work ? paugh! out upon thee! there!
Thou misbegotten sprite! was it for this! we fought and flew,
On many a bloody battle field, right on to Peterloo?

> Thou gall embittered martinet! What boots it if
> thou crack
> Thy butler's neck? Unto that lock, he'll still be
> harking back,

And grow envigorated, by thy ghastly midnight work,
Like shooting of the chutes, or breezing down the switchback
jerk!

> " Psha! that unto thee!" and I snapped my finger at
> him " bosh!

Go, give thy vengeful spirit to contrition, for the wash,
And with the soap of keen remorse, erase the stain of blood,
From out thy soul, and straight atone, with deeds of useful
good,

> Go, croak behind the Marble Arch, or take a flag
> and stand
> In Grosvenor Square, as captain of a hallelujah band,

Do anything, but mockery of murder, in the dark,
Ay even spout in windy speech, from wagons in the park,

> Thou thing of misty cobwebine! thou woman
> frighter go!

And never more be seen again, to make thyself a show.
For children's fears, or if thou would'st a manly vengeance dare,
Pick up this fourteen stone of mine, and jock me down the stair
Thou idiot spook, thou ill-conditioned cloud concocted sprite
With the immortal bard I cry, Avaunt! and quit my sight!"

So fiercely did I thus denounce, his evil midnight trick,
The vigour of the vengeful scowl upon his brow grew sick
With quail of deep abasement, to behold a mortal's blood
On fire, to beard a felon spook, and ghosts were understood,
A transposition of remorse, upon his features came,
Until he shook before me, in an abject wreck of shame,
        And cried with tones of keen reproach,

                        " Adzooks !   Alack !   Ah me !
Oddsbodikins, well well ! heigho ! that I should die to see,
My ghost derided, with contempt of scoffing stock from thee !
        But of thy clacking caustic tongue, I prithee give no
            more,
        I'll take my passage by a breeze, to-night for Singapore,
Or anywhere the wind may blow, Japan ! or Timbuctoo !
To rid me of thy clapper jaw, a flout on thee !   Adieu ! "

        He then evaporated, and with some pride embued,
        I turned, for an expression of the butler's gratitude,
But he was gone ! and from his place, with india rubber shoe,
A lamp was flashed upon my face, by number 90, Q,
        They're never where they're wanted, and that blue,
            belted elf,
        Did hail me up for trespass, and for shouting to
            myself !

Y^e Filial Sacrafice

HE was ye wrothful widowere,
      Unto his child spak he,
"Thou art not wise in this my son,
      To court with Susan Lee,
A Mayde, ye least that's prattled of,
      Ye safer for her fame,
Bethink thee, thou art Jabez Gray,
      Respect thy Sire, his name!

" Ye reputation of ye Mayde,
           Is dewdrop to ye root
Of wedded life, that canks ye blight,
           Or ripes ye wholesome fruit,
Then part thee boy, from Susan Lee,
           Her ways and lightsome game,
As Jabez Gray, behave thee well,
           Respect thy Sire, his name ! "

Ah ! well a day,
      for Jabez Gray,
O wallow
        was his woe,
It stung his heart
      with pain
           and rue,
That Mayden Lee
      should go,

Alack ! Ah ! me, that such should be,
           But compensation came,
For he was true, as Jabez Gray,
           Unto his Sire, his name.

He gave unto ye Mayde, ye sore,
             And sorry last farewell,
Ye pang unto his crinkled heart,
             Was gall of woe to tell !
But from his conscience, filial faith,
             With healing balsam came
His heart unto, for he was true,
             Unto his Sire, his name.

O then 'twas his,
     'twas Jabez Gray's
     Reward and recompense,
To hear his Sire
     bespeake ye Mayde,
In fond and future tense,

He pry'd it in ye dark of night,
             Beyond ye garden gate,
" I'll wed thee Sue, myself, to save
             Thy name from evil prate."

He heard ye Sire bespeak ye Mayde,
                    In tender guise, ye same,
As he did plead, before ye split,
                    To save ye Sire, his name.
He heard ye Parent, tell to Sue,
                    Ye lack of manly sense,
Of him, ye son, and with ye kiss,
                    He spake in future tense.

Ye little month did pass, and then,
                    Ye Parent wed ye Mayde,
And this, ye counsel to ye son,
                    In confidence he say'd,
" Ye Spinster Sue is now ye Wife,
                    Of fair and goodly fame,
Be duteous to her, as ye son
                    Respect thy Sire, his name ! "

IN BURTON Crescent,
on the semi-circle
apex there,
I lodged some little period up a six flight four foot stair,
It came about by freak of chance, 'twas in a cul-de-sac,
I found myself one morning, and compelled to tramp it back,
Whilst blessing gates of London town that bar the traffic yet,
I saw a window label, lettered, "lodgings to be let,"
A gloomy habitation 'twas, to give the nerves the creep!
But possibly a comfortable roosting place to sleep,
Of knockers on its oaken door, it bore a double stock,
I took those knockers, and I struck duet of double knock,
And just as I was rounding off my rallantando din,
The door was gently opened and a lady cried "Come in!"

c

I must confess, I fluttered with a flick of some surprise,
To see a lady so petite, and with such piercing eyes,
   An artificial bloom was on her cheek, and nose, and neck,
   Her gown was of a quaint brocade in antique floral check.
By transmutating hand of time, and his assistant care,
The golden sheen to silver light was paling thro' her hair,
   And from the dentistry of art, that crowned her rippled chin,
   She greeted me with pearly smile, the moment I stepped in.
I noted on her fingers small, some antique diamond rings,
And in her slippers russet brown, she tripped as 'twere on springs,
   A dainty wrap, completed her little quaintly self,
   She seemed a living Watteau, that stepped from off a shelf.
She seemed a living Watteau, from out a canvas sprung,
She wasn't—no, she wasn't—well you could not call her young.
   She greeted me upsmiling, with business kindled fire,
   And volunteered the question,
                  " What rooms do you require ? "
It wasn't my intention, to move upon that day,
My humor was to dawdle, in idle sort of way,
   So left it to her option, if twenty rooms or one,
   In earth upon the basement, or garret near the sun.
She showed her approbation of my eccentric style,
And greeted me politely, with confidential smile,
   " I have a room, the lodger is yet remaining there,
   But leaving soon—I'll show it, if you will step the stair.—
She mounted up before me, her little cloak, like wings,
Did supplement her flexor, and her extensor springs,
   She paused upon each lobby, to note the pleasing scene,
   Of leaves amongst the chimneys, that lent a tint of green.
The sanitary question, she settled with some pains,
Explained, the County Council had just been down the drains,

And thus discussing features, and questions to be met,
We landed on the landing of lodging to be let.
Upon the door with knuckle she struck a low rum-tin,
And tardily was answered by husky voice "Come in."
To purpose of her visit, he gave a mild assent,
Which somewhat indicated a debt of backward rent.
We entered the apartment, and gaunt, and wan, and scared!
From tangle of the blankets, blear-eyed, and towsel-haired,
A moment rose the lodger, then underneath the clothes,
He snapped himself like oyster, and only left his nose.

I took a swift synopsis, again we stepped the stair,
She bowed me to her parlour, and all around me there,
Were virtue objects, suited for curioso sale,
Art of the reign of Louis, and good old Chippendale,
Cameo ware of Wedgewood, and Worcester bric-a-brac,
Miniatures of beauties, and oriental lac,
A cabinet and tables, in marquetry of buhl,
And feminine arrangements, of bombazine and tulle.

Old mezzotint engravings of Regent, buck and lord,
Between the window curtains, an agèd harpsichord.—
The instrument she fingered, and sang an olden rune,
She sang with taste, but slightly, the strings were out of tune,
  She warbled of the Regent, of Sheridan and Burke,
  Buck Nash, and of Beau Brummel, and of the fatal work,
Enacted in a duel, then struck a broken string,
And with a sigh she faltered, and then she ceased to sing.
I told her, composition of song, was in my line,
Then, with a look intended as tender and divine,
  And mode of days of Brummel, in manner and in style,
  She lauded up the bedroom with captivating smile,
Electro-biologic, magnetic in her glance,
She fixed me like a medium, as tenant in advance !

       ✿   ✿   ✿   ✿   ✿   ✿   ✿

I entered occupation, as soon as I could get,
And everything in order, was for my comfort set,
  The room was daily garnished, and swept, my bed was made,
  In this was comprehended the lot for which I paid,
  My daily mastication, in public grill was frayed,
Monotonous, and easy, with quiet self-content,
I went and came in silence, in silence came and went,
  Was no domestic welcome when I came in, not one !
  And in the morning ditto, till I was up and gone.
No sound of brush or bucket ! no jar of door, or delph !
No foot upon the stairs, except the pair I have myself !
  No smutty wench to greet me with cloud of dusty mat !
  No snarl of vicious lap dog, or hiss of humping cat !
  No slavey whiting up the steps, did ever strike my sight !
  Yet everything was fixed for me,
               when I came home at night !

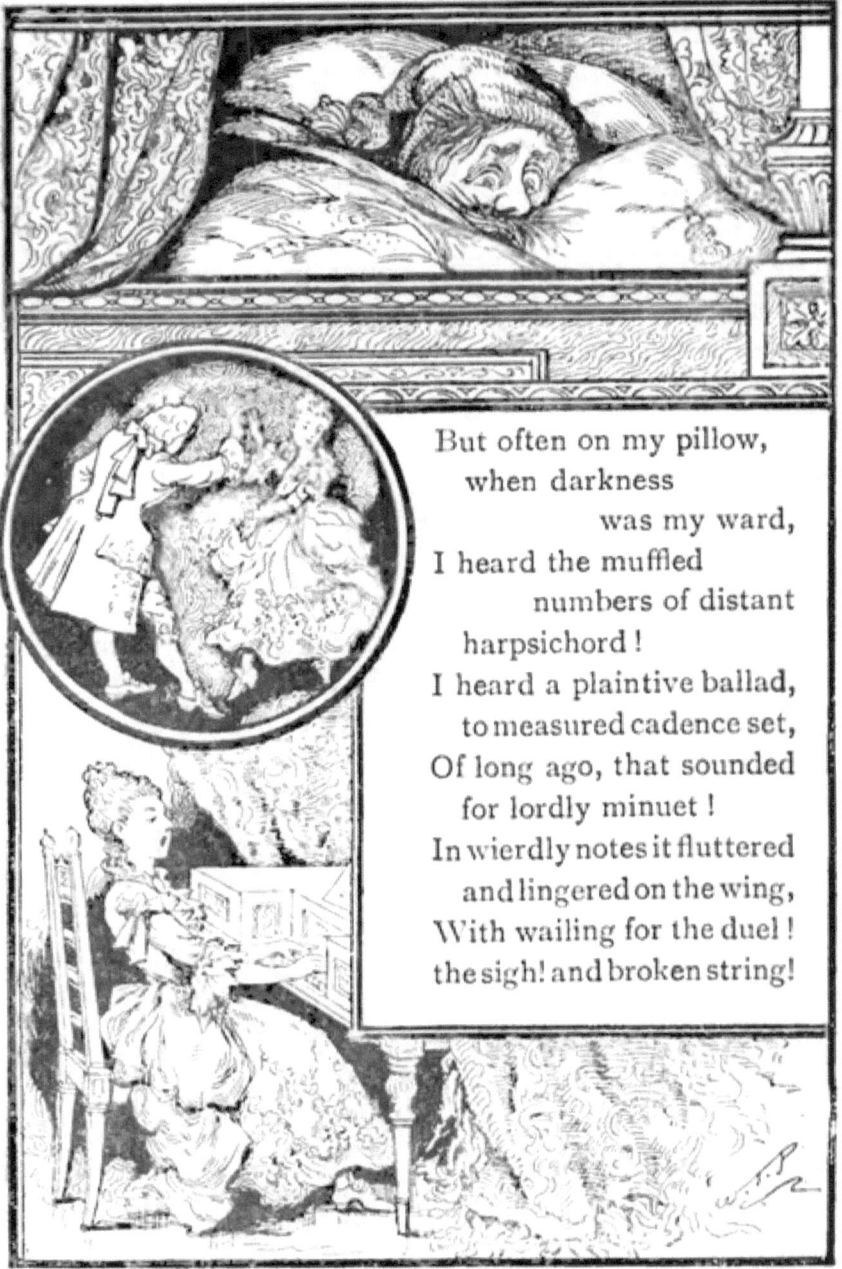

But often on my pillow,
  when darkness
            was my ward,
I heard the muffled
      numbers of distant
  harpsichord !
I heard a plaintive ballad,
  to measured cadence set,
Of long ago, that sounded
  for lordly minuet !
In wierdly notes it fluttered
  and lingered on the wing,
With wailing for the duel !
the sigh! and broken string!

*   *   *   *   *   *   *

But once when I was taking a smoking circumflex,
Around the Burton Crescent, and just at its apex,
  I heard a voice behind me, that put me on some toast,
    "Look! there's the man, that's living with Madame
      Stiffin's Ghost!"
I turned, and in the lamplight, distinctly I could see,
A woman's dexter finger, was indicating me!
    " He's living as a lodger, above the second floor
    Of yonder house, that's haunted, with double-knockered
      door,
Look! isn't he a cough-drop? it's only such a scare,
Would live in such a lodging, with Madam Stiffin there!"

I never felt so worried at anything before!
Could scarcely find the keyhole of double-knockered door,
    And up the stairs I tottered, as in a walking trance,
    Next morning, she'd be coming for payment in advance,
Next morning, at the striking of twelve upon the clock,
I started from my slumber, it was her double knock!

    I jumped up at the summons,
        and leaping out of bed,
    I answered, and she entered,
        and unto her I said,
    " I'm here thro' false pretences;
        I understand you're dead!"

    A peal of mocking laughter,
        the little Watteau shook,
And with her arms akimbo, an attitude she struck,

She made an accusation of drink, and with a glance
Of keen reproach, demanded, her payment in advance!

I had already promised myself, that none should boast,
Of knowing me in future, as tenant of a ghost,
So got my cash, pretending to settle there, and then,
And just as she was lifting my eagle pointed pen,
Said I " Perhaps you'll give me receipt for also this ? "
With that I would have tested her presence with a kiss !
I think my arm went thro' her, of that I can't be sure,
But with the table circuit, she took the bedroom door,
I took it quite as quick, and abreviated sight,
I caught of her next landing, and on her hasty flight,
From lobby down to lobby I chased her like a hare,
I tracked her to the kitchen, but lo ! she wasn't there !
I flew into the area, back up the stairs I flew,
In drawing-room and parlour, in every bedroom too,
To overtake and seize her, with skidding foot I sped,
And under every sofa, and under every bed,
I searched,—it was a marvel !—exploited every flue,
Unlocked a couple of wardrobes and looked them thro'
    and thro',
Until in all its horror, the grim conviction grew,
I had in fact been lodging unconscious with a spook !
I rushed to get my waistcoat, pants, traps, and took my hook!

HE travelled by the mail,
    On incognito scale,
        With cautious care, and reck,
            Of varied tricks of art.

For he had made a bag,
Of most extensive swag,
        From bank where he was sec.,
            And didn't want to part.

But story of his trick,
By telegraphic tick,
        Brought him to book. and check,
            It gave him quite a start,
        He had it by a neck,
            'Twas rough to have to part !

HAS been proved by more than one observant social Philosopher, that the impressionable star gazer of the Music Halls is one who often scatters rose leaves, and harvests thorns; let us hear what Muffkin Moonhead has to sing, concerning his own experience.

I T cost a florin square,
  Her photo I declare,
      To wear,
      With care
    Of uttermost esteem,
In pocket of my breast,
That picture lay at rest,
      And blest,
      With zest,
    That fluttered thro' my dream;

My dream of love, where she
Was posed, in extacy,
        Of gay phantasmagoria,
Of beauty unto me.

Ten other bobs, I pay,
For hothouse plant bouquet,
            When she,
            On tree,
        Of pantomimic treat
In semi-raiment stood,
As geni of the good,
            I could,
            And would,
        Down cast them at her feet.
The feet of love where she
Was posed, in extacy,
        Of bright phantasmagoria,
Of beauty unto me !

I took a numbered seat,
In stall select, and neat,
            To treat
            My sweet !
        And when she did appear,
I flung the flow'rs I wis,
She took them, and with this,
            O bliss
            A kiss !
        That thrilled me, while the cheer
Of gods applaudingly,

Did greet with storm of glee,
           The loved phantasmagoria
Of beauty unto me !

Sweet osculating scene
Of bouquet, and my queen,
                And smug
                Chaste hug,
           Of posies to her nose,
As poising on her toe,
And then subsiding low,
               A glow
               Flushed so,
           On my cheek, like a rose,
The while she bowed the knee,
Then skipped away O.P.,
           That lithe phantasmagoria,
Of beauty unto me !

   *   *   *   *

I waited by the door,
Classic door ! out they pour,
               A score,
               Or more,
           Escorting her, I say !
And ha ! may I be blest,
Upon each jerkin breast,
               Confest,
               Were drest,
           The buds of my bouquet !

Said she to me " ta ta !
Go home to your mamma ! "
          It wrought the rude evanishment
Of love of her from me !

The moral it is this,
Don't dally with such bliss,
          A miss,
          Is kiss
          Unto thee from the play,
A kiss for gods, and stall,
The pit, and tier, on all
          To fall
          And small
          The fig, for your bouquet,
When it has brought the balm,
Of the applauding palm,
          She shares it with the supers, and
She gives the chill to thee !

The Girl of Castlebar

THE sun was setting in a gloam of purple and gold, as I basked in the grass on the Staball hill one autumn evening, the stirring tuck of the tattoo rolled up the slope from the adjacent barracks; it affected me like a tonic, my blood circulated quicker, the spirit of an amateur ghostly seer took possession of me! I felt as one inspired. A scene of early days of Anglo-foreign strife rose before me like a wraith of second sight. The tramp of sea-bound red coats, fifes and drums, the woe-mongering cries of parting wives. I saw two lovers on the Staball hill, heard their vows.

A rhyming fever tingled to my fingers' ends, my only manuscript medium to hand, the stump of a lead pencil, and blank margin of the morning paper. Upon that virgin border I jotted the sketch of the following founded on fact ballad. The reader will perceive in it a beautiful inverse lesson of the mutual commotion of two loving hearts.

THE bugle horn was sounding through the streets of
    Castlebar,
And many a gallant soldier, was bound unto the war,
And one upon the Staball hill, his sweetheart by his side
Swore many a rounded warlike oath, that she should be his
    bride.

" O Maggie ! " cried the Corporal, " There's war across the
    sea,
And when I'm parted from thee, I would you'd pray for me,
And I will tell you what you'll do, when I am far away,
You'll come up to the Staball, and kneel for me, and pray."

And this to him she promised, and this to him she said,
" I'll still be ever true to thee, be thou alive, or dead !
I'll still be ever true to thee, and O if thou dost fall,
Thy soul at eve will find me here, upon the old Staball."

And then he swore a clinker oath, of what a vengeful doom,
Would him befal, who dared to win her from him, then the
    bloom
Came to her cheek again, " O Jim I'll never love but you,"
" I'm blowed but I'm the same ! " he cried, and then they
    tore in two !

She saw her soldier leaving, she heard the music sweet,
Of " The girl I left behind me " sounding sadly up the street,
She saw the shrieking engine, that bore him far away,
Then went back to the Staball, to weep for him and pray.

And as the summer faded, and gloaming nights came round,
A maid anon was kneeling, upon that trysting ground,
And fearless of the winter, and of its falling snow,
That maiden sweet, and constant, unto her tryst would go.

Till on a certain evening, a stranger in the town,
Came sauntering up the Staball, and found her kneeling down,
He tipped her on the shoulder, and speaking soft, and low,
" O what on earth possesses you, to pray upon the snow."

She told him all her story then, and why so kneeling there,
She told him of her sorrowed heart, the object of her prayer,
She told him of her soldier lad, so far across the sea,
" I'd like to be a soldier lad, with you to love ! " said he.

Said he " You're very lonely : If you have need to pray,
I'll come agrah ! and help you, with ' Amens ' if I may,
It's very hard acushla ! to pray alone each night,"
And the colleen shyly answered, " She thought perhaps he
    might."

The tryst became more social for while the colleen prayed,
The stranger tooted " Amens " unto the kneeling maid,
Until at last he muttered " This pantomime must stop,
I'll buy the ring to-morrow, I've got a watch to pop ! "

    *   *   *   *   *   *

At length the war was over, she heard the beaten drum,
And up again thro' Castlebar, the scarlet men did come,
And her heart grew cold within her, to think how wroth he'd
    be
To learn she had been faithless, while he was o'er the sea.

Then, pleading to her husband " O hide yerself! " she said,
" Aye even up the chimbledy, or undhernate the bed !
For if he ketches howld of you, I don't know what he'll do,
It's maybe let his gun go off, an' maybe kill the two !

I'll try an' coax the grannies, to brake it to him first,
For if he's towld it sudden by me, 'twill be the worst,
They'll have to put it softly, I cannot be his bride,
So while I'm gone to tell them, do you run off an' hide."

                                *   *   *

" O break it to him, Grannies, the shocking news," she said
" That I have wed another, and him I cannot wed !
O put it to him gently, for great will be his pain,
That we'll never more be meeting on the Staball hill again."

They broke it to him softly, 'twas in a public bar,
A foaming pint before him, and on his brow a scar,
They broke it to him gently, and spoke it to him plain,
He needn't think to meet her, on the Staball hill again.

He swigged the pint before him, then heaved a bitter sigh,
" What ? blow me, your a chaffin'! " " O divil a word o' lie ! "
Then first he took his shako, and tossed it to the roof,
Then to each nervous grannie, " Here take the bloomin' loof."

" Come, wots yer shout for liquor ? It's dooced well ! "
    cried he,
" I'm buckled to a blackimoor, I met beyond the sea,
" You've taken a load from off of me ! my mind is now at par,
She wouldn't have left a ribbon on the Girl of Castlebar ! "

VE are ze vhandering Shermans,
      Ve cooms vrom o'er ze sea,
Ve plays ze lovely music,
      Of all ze great countree,
Ve all of us have romance,
      Of life, so bigs to say,
I'll sing a verse for each man,
      Ze vile ze band vill play.

Vings zerring zanzeraza,
      Ve cooms from o'er ze sea,
Ve plays ze lovely music,
      Of all ze great countree.

Zare's Herr Von Zingerpofel,
      No prouder man vos he,
Zan ven he loved ze Fraulien
      Afar in Shermanie.
But ven he found ze noders
      Golds ring upon her hand,
He played on ze thriangles,
      Und left ze Sherman land!

Zare's Blunder Bogle Fogen,
      Vot bangs on ze big dhrum,
Thought all ze poor, und rich man,
      Should own ze even sum ;
Ze government vos differed,
      But on ze prison valks,
He doubled up ze gaoler,
      Und zen, he valked ze chalks !

Zare's Dreker Mandertoofel,
      Ze opheclide he plays,
He'll never more see nodings,
      Of all his happiest days ;
He only blows ze music,
      Because it brings ze cheer,
Of great big pipes of shmokin',
      Und shugs of Lager Beer !

Zare's him vot puffs ze oboe,
      In oder days vos he,
Of Heidelberg, a student
      Ze pride of Shermanie,
But he did love der Lager,
      Zoo mooch of Docter-Vien,
He killed ze man in duel !
      Und he vos no more seen.

Zare's Mungen Val Tarara,
      A Sherman born in Cork,
Und he vos von too many,
      Because he vould not vork,

He left his home von mornings,
      Mit all his back hair curled,
He jangs upon ze cymbals,
      To bring him round ze vorld.

Now you vill be imagine,
      Zat I must oondherstand,
Zat I vill tell ze story
      Of leader of ze band,
But if I must, I'll speaks it,
      All in ze simple rune,
So I vill stop ze music,
      Ze tale is out of tune!

'Twas I vos vonce a Uhlan, who rode mit all ze band,
Zat von Alsace, und Lorraine, from Vrance vor Vaterland,
Ven in ze pits at Gravelotte, I lay von night to die,
I voke! for I vos faintings to hear ze voman sigh!

Und shust vere I vas vounded, I saw ze voman's zere,
Vos bound mine arm from bleeding, mit her own golden hair!
She nursed me through ze danger, und ven zere's peace again,
I svore zat I vould ved her, ze Fraulein of Lorraine.

I kissed my love von mornings, her vite face on my heart,
Mit sobs her eyes vos veeping, ze time vos come to part.
Ze Var vas not yet ended, I heard ze thrompet blow,
Zat I must rise, und answer, und leave ze sveetheart so!

Mine blood run cold zat mornings, und I felt somedings here,
Vos in my throat come choking, und on my cheek ze tear,
Vor O I vould not lose her, ze glory on me now,
Zat I vos hope to bless me, mit Cosette vor mine Frau.

I marched avay to Paris, vere all around vos dire,
Mit shmoke, und blood, und thunder, und fret, und woe und
    fire!
Und ven ze siege vos over, mit thrumpet und mit dhrum,
Vonce more again thro' Lorraine, ze Sherman bands did come.

I vent to find ze sveetheart, but grass vos on ze slain,
Ze cruel Var had murdered ze Fraulein of Lorraine!—
Shust vere mine heart is beating, I keep ze treasure zare,
Mit mine own blood upon it, von braid of golden hair,
Und all dried up und vithered, und gone to dust again,
Von flower zat vonce vos jewelled ze grave zats in Lorraine.

Ah vot is deed of glory, ven blood is on ze vings
Of love, zat makes ze heaven on earth, und vot are kings?
Auch! I vill have no patience. Strike up ze Band again,
Or I grow mad mit dhreamings, vot happened in Lorraine!

Vings zerring zanzaraza, ve cooms from o'er ze sea,
Ve plays ze lovely music, of all ze great countree.
Ve all of us have romance of life so bigs to say,
Vings zerring zanzaraza, ze vile ze band vill play.

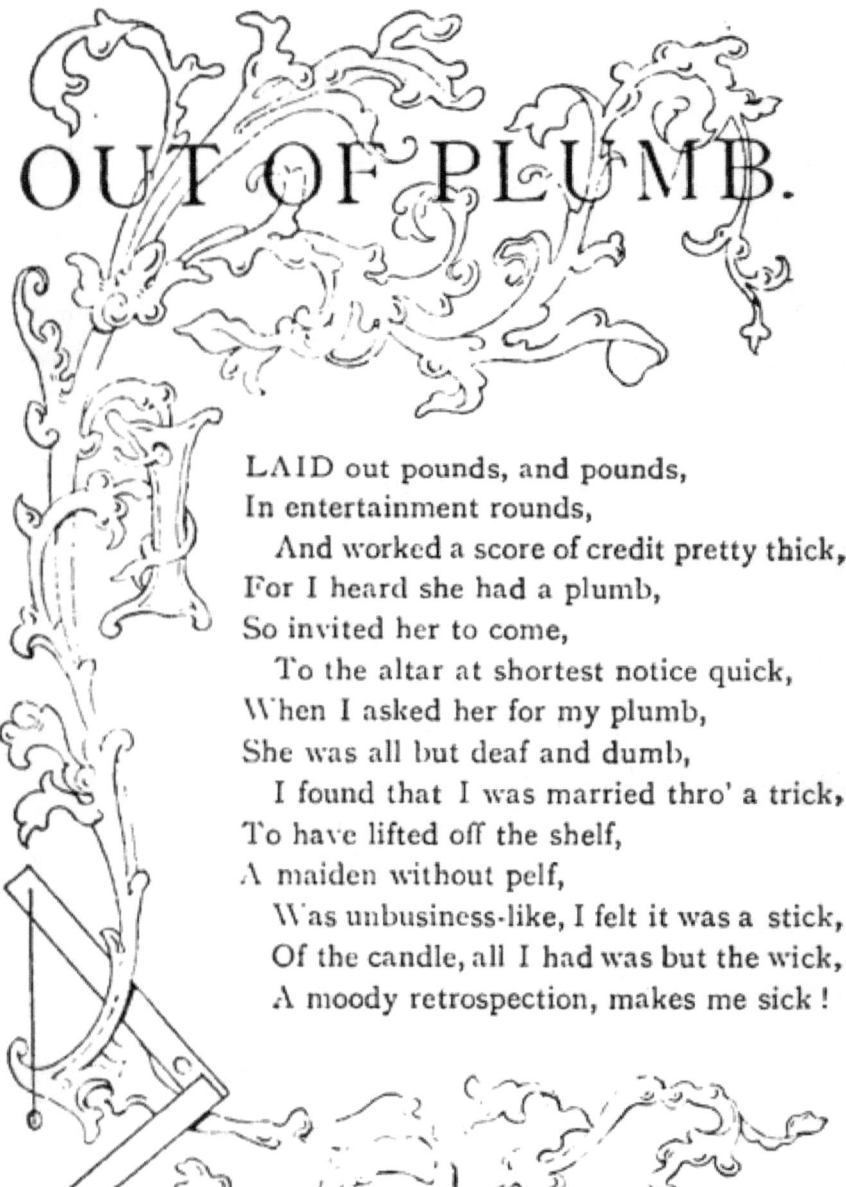

OUT OF PLUMB.

LAID out pounds, and pounds,
In entertainment rounds,
    And worked a score of credit pretty thick,
For I heard she had a plumb,
So invited her to come,
    To the altar at shortest notice quick,
When I asked her for my plumb,
She was all but deaf and dumb,
    I found that I was married thro' a trick,
To have lifted off the shelf,
A maiden without pelf,
    Was unbusiness-like, I felt it was a stick,
    Of the candle, all I had was but the wick,
    A moody retrospection, makes me sick !

A Ward in The Chancerie

HE WAS a cabman grey I feck,
  All weird and wry to see;
His face was ribbed like the turtle's neck,
  His nose like the strawberrie.
If you think he was old, to you I say,
  Your thought obscures the truth—
Despite the years that had passed away,
  He was still in his second youth.

" Ha ! ha ! " quoth he, " how fair she looks,"
  One morn, as he did see,
A maiden sweet with her school-books,
  A ward in the Chancerie.
" How fair she looks ! " quoth he, and put
  A load in his old black clay,
And he didn't care if he hadn't a fare,
  The whole of the live-long day.

That night
he looketh into the glass,
    With his nose
like a strawberrie,
      "I know they'll say
I'm a bloomin' goose
But fate is fate you see."
      And he looketh
into the glass once more,
    Where yet
was another drain.
Quoth he, "I've wedded three before,"
"The fourth I'll wed again."

Next day he was out in the open street,
    And standing upon the stand,
He heard the trip of her coming feet,
    'Twas sweet as a German band.
And forth he went and accosted her,
    He could not brook delay,
"Hey up, look here, little gurl," said he,
    "I saw you yesterday."

"I saw you yesterday.   My 'eart
    Went out across your feet,
And from your beauty came a dart
    That fixed me all complete;
And all last night I dreamed a dream,
    To my bedside you came—
You'll marvel at these words of him
    Who does not know your name.

" I saw you yesterday.   You smile."
  His eyes, like burning beads,
Took root in her inmost soul the while,
  As deep as the ditch-grown weeds.
" You smile.   Ha, ha ! to smile and laugh
  Is better than aye to frown
It's fitter to whiffle away the chaff
  That covers a golden crown.

" It's better to whittle away the cheat
  Of mankind if you can."
And he cracked his whip.   " It's a fair deceit
  And I am a curious man—
Yes I am a curious man, my badge
  Is seventeen seventy-seven,
But wot is a badge ?   It's a very small thing
  To the matches wot's made in Heaven ! "

" How sweet he speaks ! "
  the maiden thought
" He's a lord
  in a rough disguise,
As a cabman old
  he's coming to woo
And give me
  a grand surprise ;

He seeks to hide himself in a mask,
  With a nose like a strawberrie,
But I've read too many of three vol. novs.,
  He couldn't disguise from me.

" The Lord of Burleigh while incog.
  Did wed an humble bride,
And legend lore recounteth more
  Of love like his beside.
I've heard the ballad of Huntingtower,
  And some I forget by name,
And when he's got rid of his strawberrie nose
  He'll maybe be one of the same. ! "

And she fondly looked on him, I ween,
  Sweet as the hawthorn spray,
When all in bloom of white and green,
  It decks the month of May.

"Oh, dearest Cabman," spoke she then,
  " No brighter fate were mine
Than this : to be thine own laydee,
  My life with thee to twine.

" But I am poor and lowly born,
  And never a match for thee—
A girl a man like you would scorn,
  A ward in the Chancerie,
With only a hundred thousand pounds,
  It may be less or more ;
But do not wreck a confiding heart,
  It often was done before."

" Wo ! ho !" quoth he, and in his sleeve
  He grinned, " It's a big mistake.
The Chancerie is only a blind,
  But, yet, I am wide awake.

If a hundred thousand pounds wor her's,
    She wouldn't be makin' free;
I'd have to court her a little bit more,
    Before she'd be courtin' me.

" I haven't the smallest doubt of this—
    The truth you tell," he began ;
" But I think that you misunderstand me miss,
    I am not a marryin' man.
I only thought if you wanted a cab
    That I wouldn't be high in my fare,"
And he shuffled the nose-bag round the jaw
    Of his patient, hungry mare.

She walked away, nor bade good day,
    While he thought of the Probate Court.
" She's a girl, I twig, could give me a dig
    Of a barrister's wig for sport.

I have only escaped
        the courts of law,"
Quoth he,
        " by a single hair ! "
As he finished the knot
        of his canvas bag
On the nose
        of his hungry mare.

The Hair Queen

M ANY an intelligent reader will perceive that the following is a pathetic plaint founded on fact. A moral, conveyed in a polyglot sample of weak passages from many a knowing man's career.

In one noted instance, the writer while reciting the ballad, closely escaped the chance of assassination, at the hand of a member of the audience, that he fancied it was a versification of his own particular experience, made public, and brought so circumstantially home to him, that he felt the eyes of all were concentrated upon him as the hero of the ballad. Happily he did not carry a revolver, or it would most likely have exploded suddenly in the direction of the platform. But mutual explanations and further enquiry elicited the information that more than one man of that audience occupied the same lamplit boat of retrospect misfortune.

Corney Keegan relates his adventure with the picturesque force, derived from practical experience, and many an aching heart will go out to him in sympathy. His story teaches a comprehensive, solemn, and beautiful lesson.

M E mother often spoke to me,
        " Corney me boy," siz she,
" There's luck in store for you agra !
        You've been so kind to me !
Down be the rath in Reilly's Park
        They say that Larry Shawn
That's gone away across the say,
        Once cotch a Leprechawn.

He grabbed him be the scruff so hard,
        The little crather swore,
That if bowld Larry'd let him go,
        He should be poor no more !
" Just look behind ye Larry dear,"
        Screeched out the chokin' elf,
" There's hapes of goold in buckets there,
        It's all for Larry's self !
" If Larry lets the little man
        Go free again, he'll be
" No longer poor but rich an' great ! "
        So Larry let him free.
Some say he carried home the goold
        An' hid it in the aves,
But some say when the elf was gone
        'Twas turned to withered laves

" If Larry cotch a Leprechawn,"
        Me mother then 'ed cry,
" Why you may ketch a fairy queen,
        Ma bouchal by an' by ! "

Near Balligarry now she sleeps,
  Where great O'Brien bled,
And often since I took a thought,
  Of what me mother said.

At last I came to Dublin town,
  To thry an' sell some pigs,
And maybe then I didn't cut
  A quare owld shine of rigs.
I sowld me pigs for forty pound,
  For they wor clane an' fat,
An' thin we hadn't American mate,
  So they wor chape at that !

" Well now," sez I, " me pocket's full,
  I'll not go home just yit,
I'll take a twist up thro' the town
  An' thrate meself a bit,"
I mosey'd round to Sackville Street,
  When starin' round me best,
I seen a darlin' colleen there,
  Most beautifully dhressed.

A posy in her leghorn hat,
  An' round her neck, a ruff
Of black cock's feathers, jacket too,
  Of raal expensive stuff.
A silver ferruled umberell'
  In hand with yalla kid,
An' thro' a great big hairy muff
  Her other hand was hid,

O like a sweet come-all-ye, in
     A waltzin' swing, she swep'
The toepath, with the music of
     Her silken skirt, an' step,
To see her turn the corner, thro'
     The lamplight comin' down,
You'd think she owned
               the freehowld of
     That part of Dublin town!
You'd think she owned
               the sky above,
     It's moon with all the stars,
The thraffic in the streets below,
     Their thrams, an' carts,
               an' cars!
You'd think that she
               was landlady,
     Of all that she could see,
An' faith regardin' of meself,
     She made her own of me!

"O Corney is it you ? " siz she,
   An' up to me she came,
I took a start, to hear her there,
   Pronouncin' out me name ;
" O Corney, there ye are ! " siz she
   Wid raal familiar smile,
An' thin begar she took me arm,
   Most coaxingly the while ;

I fluttered like a butterfly,
   That's born the first of May,
Wid pride, as if I had the right
   Hand side, the Judgment Day!
I felt as airy as a lark that
   Skies it from the ground,
To think she'd walk wid me, poor chap,
   Wid only forty pound !

She took me arm, an' thrapsed wid me,
   All down be Sackville Sthreet,
An' colleens beautifully dhressed,
   In two's and three's, we meet,
An' men that grinned, a greenish grin,
   Of envy from their eye,
To see me wid that lady grand,
   Like paycock marchin' by.

Till comin' to a lamp, I turned,
   An' gazed into her eyes,
Me heart that minute took me throat
   Wid lump of glad surprise,

E

Siz I, " Me jewel, thim two eyes,
   Are sparklin' awful keen,
" I'm sure," siz I, " I've come across,
   Me mother's Fairy Queen ! "
"O Corney yis," siz she, " I am,
   A Fairy Queen ; " siz she,
" An' I can make yer fortune now,
   If you'll just come with me."
Wid that, I ups and says " of coorse ! "
   As bowld as I could spake,
" An' sure I will me darlin', if
   Its only for your sake."

Well, whin we passed the statutes white,
   Up to O'Connell Brudge,
The Fairy Queen
   smiled up at me,
An' gev a knowin' nudge,

:" Corney ! " siz she, " I want a dhrink ! "
   " Do ye me dear ? " siz I,
An' on the minute faith I felt,
   Meself was shockin' dhry.

Well then she brought me coorsin off,
   Down be the Liffy's walls,
An' up a narra gloomy sthreet,
   Up to a Palace Halls !
An' there they wor, all splindid lit,
   " Come in me love," siz she.
I thought me heart 'ed brake, to hear
   Her spake so kind to me !
Well in we wint, an' down we sat,
   Behind a marvel schreen,
An' there we dhrank, of drink galore,
   Me an' the Fairy Queen.
She spoke by alphabetic signs,
   Siz she, " We'll have J.J.
An' whin we swalley'd that, siz she,
   " L.L. is raal O.K."

We tossed them off like milk, siz she,
   " At these we need'nt stick,
D. W. D.'s a quench you'll find,
   A. 1, an' up to Dick ! "
Well thin she left the alphabet,
   An' flying to the sky,
" The three star brand's the best " siz she,
   " To sparkle up your eye,"
Thin " here ! " says she " just taste Owld Tom,"
   But augh ! agin me grain

E2

It wint ! siz she " It's mum's the word,
          We'll cure it, wid champagne ! "
I never drank such sortin's, of
          The drink, in all me life,
Signs on it, in the mornin', me
          Digestion, was at strife !

At last, we qualified our drooth,
          An' up she got, siz she,
" We'll just retire to private life,
          So Corney, come wid me."
But just before I stood to go,
          I siz quite aisy " Miss,
You might bestow poor Corney K.
          One little simple kiss."

" Ah ! Corney tibbey, sure," said she,
          " Two if ye like, ye thrush ! "
O have ye saw the blackberries,
          Upon the brambly bush ?
The Johnny Magory still is bright,
          Whin all the flowers are dead,
Her hair, was like the blackberries !
          Her dhress, Magory red !

O have you ever saunthered out
          Upon a winther's night,
Whin the crispy frost, is on the ground,
          An' all the stars, are bright ?
Then have you bent your awe sthrick gaze,
          There, up aginst the skies ?
The stars are very bright, you think,
          Well thim was just her eyes

Were you ever down at the strawberry beds,
      An' seen them dhrowned in chrame?
Well that was her complexion, and
      Her teeth, wor shockin' white!
An' the music of her laughin' chaff,
      Was like a beggar's dhrame,
Whin he hears the silver jingle, and
      His rags are out of sight!

I thought the dhrop of dhrink was free,
      But throth I had to pay!
I thought it quare, but then I thought,
      It was the fairy's way;
" Howld on " siz I, " she's thryin' me,
      Have I an open heart,
Before she makes me fortune," so,
      Begar! I took a start
Of reckless generosity,

    An' flung me money round,
'Twas scatthered on the table!   In
    Her lap, an' on the ground!
I seen it glitter in the air,
    Before me wondherin' eyes,
Like little yalla breasted imps,
    All dhroppin from the skies!
O then I knew that it was threw,
    She was a Fairy Queen,
The goold, came dhroppin'! whoppin'! hoppin'
    The like was never seen!
I gave a whipping screech of joy!
    Whin, wid a sudden whack,
Some hidden wizard, riz his wand,
    An' sthruck me from the back,
Down came the clout upon the brain,
    An' froze me senses quite,
An' over all me joy at once,
    There shot the darkest night!

 *   * *   *

I knew no more, till I awoke,
    An' found meself alone,
I thrust me hand, to grasp me purse,
    Me forty pounds wor gone!
O then, with awful cursin', if
    I didn't raise the scenes,
" Bad luck! " siz I, " to Leprechauns,
    Bad scran, to Fairy Queens!
Bad luck to them, that spreads abroad,
    Such shockin' lyin' tales,
Bad scran has me, that tears me hair,

An' forty pounds bewails ! "
With that, I seen a man, come up,
        A dark arch, marchin' thro',
As if he hadn't any work,
        Particular to do.
He measured me, wid selfish eye,
        As cat regards a rat,
An' whin he spoke, begor I found,
        'Twas just his price at that !
Siz he " What's all this squealin' for ?
        What makes ye bawl ? " siz he,
Siz he, " I'm a dissective, so,
        You'll have to come wid me ! "
Siz he, " Yer shouts wor almost loud
        Enough, to crack the delph !
An' in the mornin' I must bring
        Ye up, before himself ! "
" Arrah ! What for ? " siz I, an' thin,
        I towld him all me woe,
An' how I woke, an' found meself
        Asleep, an' lyin' low.
I towld him of the whipsther, that
        Had whipped me forty pound,
An' left me lyin' fast asleep,
        In gutther, on the ground.
Then leerin' like, he turned, and siz,
        " You're a nice boy ! complate !
To go wid Fairy Queens, like that,
        An' lose yer purse, so nate.
Corney ! " siz he, " go home ! " siz he,
        " She might have sarved ye worse,

I'll thry me best, to ketch the Fay,
> An' get you back yer purse.
But look! don't shout like that again,
> It was a shockin' shout,
It sthruck me, 'twas a house a-fire!
> You riz up such a rout.

I thought you'd wake me wife! she sleeps,
> Down in a churchyard near!"
Wid that, the dark dissective turned,
> An' bursted in a tear!
I dhribbled out a few meself,
> Me brow, wid shame I bint,
An' like a lamb, from slaughter, slow,
> Wid tottherin' steps I wint,
But never, never from that day,
> Was any tidins' seen,
Of me owld purse, me forty pound!
> Or of the Fairy Queen!

Then, whin I thought of Norah's wrath,
> An' what a power she'd say,
Me fine black hair, riz on me skull,
> An' grew all grizzle gray!
O never more, to Dublin town,
> I'll come, to sell me pigs!
I walk a melancholy man,
> Like one, that's got the jigs,
An' in the town of Limerick, if
> You ever chance, to meet
A haggard man, wid batthered hat,
> Come sthridin down the sthreet,

An' if he stops, by fits and starts,
                An' stares at nothin' keen !
Say "there goes Corney, look he's mad !
                He cotch a Fairy Queen."
And if you chance in Sackville Sthreet,
                Or any other way,
To meet, all beautifully dhrest,
                A lovely colleen gay ;

An' if she chances on the name,
                That you wor christened by,
An' laughs, as if she knew ye,
                With a cute acquaintance eye,
An' if she takes your arm, an' siz,
                That she's a Fairy Queen,
Start back in horror, shout aloud,

                O woman am I green !
Am I before a doctor's shop,
                Where coloured bottles be ?
Is there a green light, on my face,
                That you should spake to me ?
Go home, O Fairy Queen, go home !
                At once, an' holus bolus !
Remimber, Corney Keegan's purse,
                An' think of the Dublin Polis

The Devil in Richmond Park

I was walking about, in a
casual way,
Thro' the ferns, in Richmond
Park,
'Twas just at the fringe of the
twilight hour,
On the skirt, of the time
called dark,
And the wind was rough, and I
couldn't succeed,
To kindle my three-
penny smoke,
When a gentleman stepped
from behind a tree,
And coughed, and
hemmed, and
spoke :

" You'll pardon me, Sir, you're in want of a light,"
    Said he, with a bow to me,
And straight producing a braided star,
    He struck it against his knee,
And with an expression of much concern,
    To see that my weed was right,
He manipulated the light himself,
    With a courtesy most polite.

I am one, who is quickly impressed, and won,
    By measure of courteous act,
So deeming it right, to appreciate,
    In response of appropriate tact,
I spake to him thus, " It's rare that a man
    In a gentleman's dress like thine,
Doth care to assist, the frivolous wants,
    Of a miniature vice like mine,
So reckon it not, as a rudeness wrought,
    Of an ignorant wish to know,
But I'd certainly like to learn the name,
    Of the gent, who has touched me so !

Then he glittered a grin, from his cat-like eye,
    Thro' a coal black lash on me,
And he bowed, with his lifted silk top hat,
    " I'm the Devil himself ! " quoth he.

Good gracious ! yes, I was certainly struck,
    So suddenly thus to be
With the Devil himself ! but soon, or late,
    He was bound to appear to me.

So screwing my nerves, to concert pitch,
    To play up my soul, for wealth,
With a supplemental proviso made,
    For excellent mortal health,
I offered to scribble my autograph,
    In blood, old-storied style,
To deed, for a compensating line,
    From his notable strong room pile.

But he looked on me, with a pitying glance,
    I counted somewhat queer,
And answered me thus,—in a friendly way,
    With a slight sarcastic leer.

T'S a long time, Sir, I assure you,
    since
    I endeavoured, to so combine,
My games of spoof, for the human
    soul,
    In the bartering oofftish line.
I suffered by many a measly cheat,
    When mortals made those sales,
You'll read of their shuffling knavish
    tricks,
    Thro' the mediæval tales,
If you think, that by selling your soul to me,
    Is the way to get rich, it ain't,
You'll have to become, a Devil yourself,
    In the garb, of a modern Saint.

" It's the fashionable way, to play the game,
    Of hypocritical spoof,
You have only to tailor your saintly robe,
    To cover your tell tale hoof,
You have only to hypnotise mankind,
    And teach them, to gaze on high,
And while you have mesmerised them thus,
    With eyes, to the upward sky,

" You can plot, exploit, and sneak, and trick,
    And cram your wallet, with wares,
And earthly stocks, as you boom the run,
    On the New Jerusalem shares,
You can rob the widow, and orphan child ;
    But reputably go to church,
And if, by the clogging of circumstance,
    Your pinched, in the doomdock lurch,
The greater the pile of swag, you've made,
    The fewer the blanks, you'll draw,
From the lottery wheel, of the English bench,
    In the name, of the English law.
It's merely a mode, of paying yourself,
    In advance, a liberal wage,
For the government work, you'll have to do,
    In the broad-arrow-branded stage.
Say thirty thousands of pounds, you filch,
    Five years, is the time you'll do,
Six thousand a year, in advance, you see,
    To enjoy, when you've pulled it thro'.
Or, seizing your pile, by a dextrous coup,
    Before they have time, to look down,

From the castles, in the air,
You have built for them there,
    You can take a foreign ticket from town.
" And tho' you are lagged, at the ends of the earth,
    You'll still find a breach, or a flaw,
Whereby you can slip, thro' the quips, that confuse,
    Extradition—international law.

" Now that is how I teach, the quickest way to cure,
    Your impecuniosity complaint,
You must collar the swag, as a Devil yourself,
    In the garb, of a modern saint.
There's another way to pinch, whereby you may keep,
    Your character, apparently sound,
Go pray, and exhort, teach the vanity of wealth,
    And pay, half-a-crown in the pound !

" Now bear it in mind, if you're wanting to make,
    Let this, be your measureless plaint,
The misery of wealth, get a halo, and preach,
    In the garb, of a modern Saint."

Again he lifted his silk top hat,
    And bowing an adieu to me,
He vanished away, with a lordly crawl,
    In the trunk, of the nearest tree,
And thus, were my mediaeval hopes
    Of wealth, by a caustic blow,
Dispersed, and a lesson of evil taught,
    By the Devil, who touched me so.

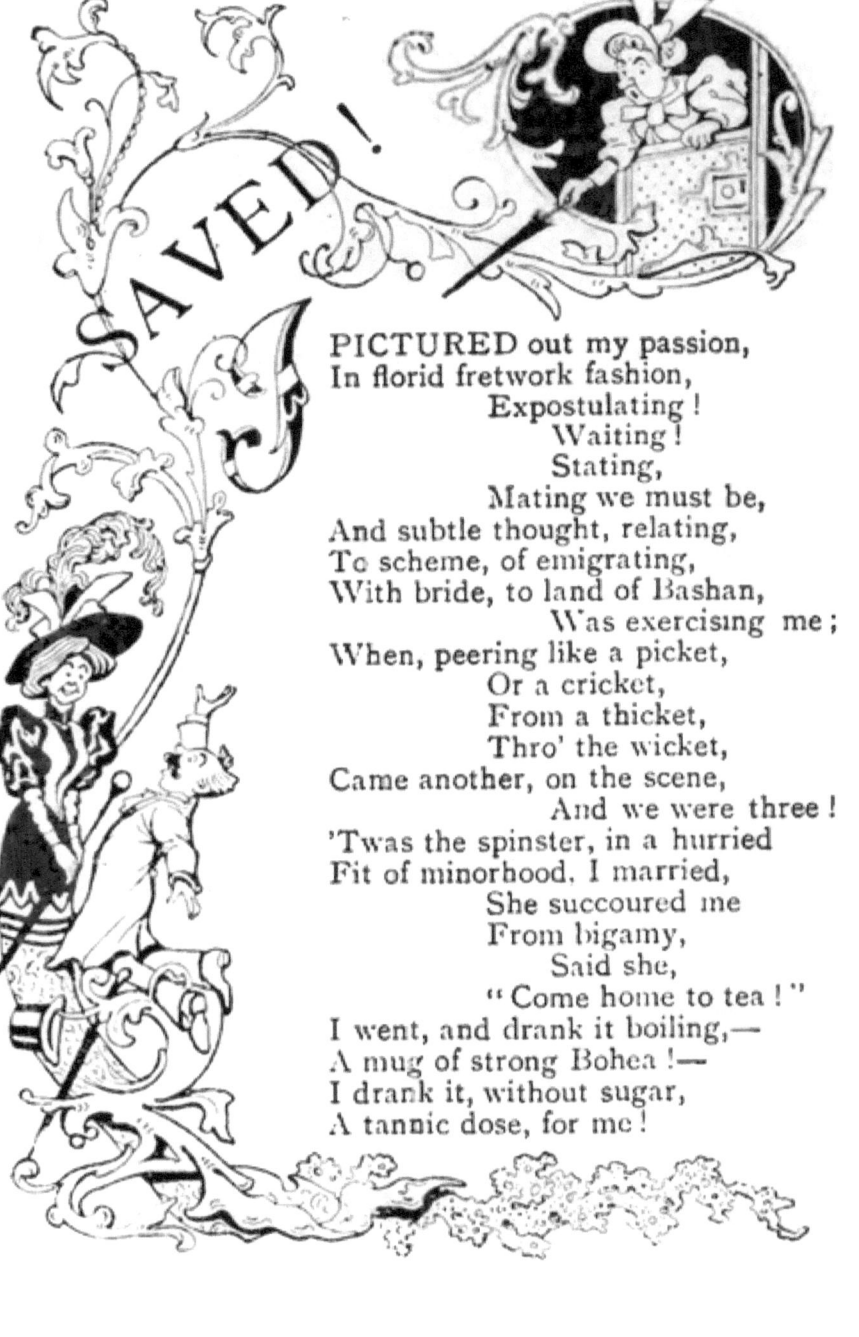

SAVED!

PICTURED out my passion,
In florid fretwork fashion,
  Expostulating!
   Waiting!
   Stating,
  Mating we must be,
And subtle thought, relating,
To scheme, of emigrating,
With bride, to land of Bashan,
    Was exercising me;
When, peering like a picket,
   Or a cricket,
   From a thicket,
   Thro' the wicket,
Came another, on the scene,
    And we were three!
'Twas the spinster, in a hurried
Fit of minorhood. I married,
   She succoured me
   From bigamy,
    Said she,
  "Come home to tea!"
I went, and drank it boiling,—
A mug of strong Bohea!—
I drank it, without sugar,
A tannic dose, for me!

'TWAS an incident Matrimonial,
    the Probate Court the place,
And 'twas for the co-respondent, a most
    remarkable case,
For good was the leading counsel, and moral
    the words spake he,
And fashionable ladies listened, to Writ
    MacFee, Q.C.

He rose to his feet and setting his most
    magniloquent frown,
He fingered his brief for a moment, a
    moment, and laid it down,
Then out of his golden snuff box, he powdered
    his pampered nose,
And then with a pull back rustle of silk, to
    its wonted pose,
He heliographed to the jury, a glitter of eyeful glee,
And as he surveyed the respondent, most rep-re-hen-siv-lee,
He mounted his golden pinc-nez, and on this wise spake he.

"Me Lud, and O gents of the Jury, it's a most remarkable case!
And I don't hesitate for a moment, my cause in your hands
    to place,
For O," said the counsellor, purring, with subtle seductive leer,
" I never beheld such a jury, in the length of my long career !
I assure you it makes it easy for an advocate like to me,
To open the most remarkable case *ver*. Tommins, L.R.C.P."

Then marking his condemnation, with voice like a double
    bass D.
" The co-respond' is a doctor, John Tommins, L.R.C.P.,
A leech of the muddiest water, a pill, that has given the sick,
An emetic of truth, a plaister of pitch, with a warrant to stick,
It's O when consumptive virtue, is treated by such, you see
The ruin, like that enacted by Tommins, L.R.C.P.

He was called to attend the Lady May Monica Pendigrew,
From a fit of the blues he roused her, and prettily pulled her
    through,
But managed her like a pilot, who getting a treacherous grip,
Sails out into deeper water, to scuttle and sink the ship !
O gents, by æsthetical fraud, he played on the lady's mind,
With Shakespeare collar and fur, a sunflower, and such kind,
He called her too utterly too, and posed in a limpish style,
And droned in a minorly key, of love, like a fretwork file.
Me Lud, and O gentlemen, gents, the co-respond' may smile,
Your sympathy thus to win, by means of trover of guile,
But no ! you will give him a check, whereby you will take
    your place,
As the most remarkable twelve, of the most remarkable case ! "

'Twas thus, with vigour, and vim, and verve, and casuist glee,
The raftered roof re-echoed, the shouts of Writ MacFee,
While envious briefless Bees, admired his logic, and gist,
Accentuate note, and pause, well marked by his thumping fist,
He stood on the councillor's seat, with one of his feet—the left,
And the stuffy compression of air, with whirling silk he cleft,
And this, was his winding up, " O Father, Brother, and Son,
Oh this is a case, concerning each individual one,
And confident of your verdict, now into your hands I place,
O gentlemen, gents of the Jury, this most remarkable case ! "

With quiver of deep emotion, one hypnothetical glance,
He photophoned to the jury, at Tommins he looked askance,
Then daintily mopped his forehead, some virtuous beads of heat,
He sopped in his red bandana, and then he resumed his seat.

Then " Oh ! " said the ladies in court,
                    " Wasn't that lawyer a treat ? "

Concussion of parasols, sticks, hands, and stamping feet,
Till the usher expostulated, aloud in a startling shout,

"Silence ! ! !"

And his Ludship sternly threatened, to bundle the audience out,

Poor Tommins had then to listen
to evidence from the box,
And now, and again, it dealt him,
a stagger of nasty knocks ;
Acquaintances there subpœnad,
identification swore,
And others, who sneaked the keyhole, of sitting apartment door.
What mattered the osculation,
with which he smacked the
book,
A fig for his indignation, a jot for
his injured look,
The jury, and judge, decided the
damage, and costs, to be

Three thousand pounds, to the client of Writ MacFee, Q.C.

✲   ✲   ✲   ✲

THE tweezers of time, had sparsed his hair, when
    Tommins, L.R.C.P.

Was mooning around, to a neighbouring square, to join in an
    evening tea,

When a tremulous maiden, checked his steps, and cried him,
    "O Mister Man,

Me mother's afeered, that the two pair back, is goin' to kick
    the can !

O Mister Medical Sir, he's sick, an' owin' a quarter's rent,

An' that's the most, of the cause for why, of the hurry, that I
    was sent,

O Mister Medical Man, Sir please, O please Sir folly me
    quick,

You might be able to worry him thro' from the fit of the
    stiffnin' sick ! "

Oh ! come Sir, please Sir, do Sir come,

O hurry an' come with me quick ! "

From sympathetic professional heart,
    for indigent sick alway,

He gave a positive kind response, to
    the girl, who thus did pray,

And on thro' court, and alley, and lane,
    he followed her devious track,

Then mounting a rickety deal wood
    stair, he entered a two pair back,

And there, in the glim of a halfpenny
    dipt, he gazed on a ghastly man,

And he counted his pulse, said the
    girl " Do you think he's likely to
    kick the can ? "

The sick man rose to an elbow prop, at Tommins, to blink
    and stare!
He seemed an anatomy, made for show, of eyes, and nose, and
    hair,
He peered awhile thro' the starving glim, and then, with a
    moan cried he,

" O God, have you come to haunt me here, John Tommins,
    L.R.C.P. ?
O is it with pills, or senna and salts, your 'shake up the bottle'
    and mess
Of slops, to avenge for the deed I've done ? have mercy and
    I'll confess !
O pester me not to swallow your stuff, I will not allow you to
    bleed !
O spare me Tommins, I'm guilty, guilt, is what I'm about to
    plead ! "

The doctor shrank with a searching gaze, that clung to the
    startled ghost,
In doubt awhile, for the rounded lines of his manhood's prime
    were lost,
Till memory striking the evil past, the doctor's eye did trace,
With a shock to his heart, the Writ MacFee of the most
    remarkable case !
His memory jarred on the Probate Court, with all its
    sorrowful shame,
Disastrous check, to his early hopes, of honor, and medical
    fame,
And with a potion of pity, and hate, he knew the furrowy face
Of the grim, of the Writ MacFee, Q.C., of the most remark-
    able case.

The bloom of his pampered nose was gone, 'twas shrivelled, and pinched, and shrunk!

His adipose peach of cheek, was fled, 'twas lean, and withered, and sunk,

A derelict there; by the prosperous port of wealth, and power, and place,

He lay the identical Writ MacFee, of the most remarkable case!

" O spare me doctor! for I'll confess,—I should have been in your place.

As the treacherous co-respondent, of the most remarkable case,

T'was I, was the homestead wrecker, but never as Writ MacFee.

I played me, a knave's deception, as Tommins, L.R.C.P.!

I bought from a needy super, the beard, moustaches, and wig,

I managed to coach my tailor, to model me in your rig,

And thus I received a welcome, to lunch, and dinner, and tea,

As Tommins the medical doctor, but never as Writ MacFee.

O Doctor Tommins have mercy! I beg to legacy thee,
With thirty tickets of pawn to name, of Writ MacFee, Q.C.
In a brief bag under the bed, tied up in a worn-out wig,
You will find a memento there, of mock æsthetical rig,
The spats and the collar and vest, I wore when I went to see,
The Lady Monica Pendigrew, as Tommins, L.R.C.P.
O Doctor Tommins forgive! the cost and the foul disgrace,
Of debt, for the illsome guilt, of the most remarkable case,
O Doctor Tommins have grace!" he rose with a greedy stare,
And gripped with his reedy fists, the mat of his weedy hair!
Then moaning a hungry sigh, for life, with a choking breath,
He fell with accusing cry, "O Tommins you've brought
    me death!
But I won't have a pauper's coffin! so give me a decent show—
Whew!—eh—what's this? O thunder thun—un—der and
    lightning———————————Oh!
Ah!—mercy me Lud! O mercy! thun—un—der an' light—
    ning———————Oh!!
It's a sine die, the morrow for me, Ah! mercy me Lud, Oh!———
    ————————Oh!

The girl ran out of the two pair back, and down the stairs
    she ran,
With shouts, as she took three steps at a time, " The lodger
    has kicked the can!
Mother, O mother, we've lost the rent, the lodger has kicked
    the can!
It's just what you said of the two pair back, he's gone an
    he's kicked the can!"

A Tour to Svitserland

AID she, " The Parkinses have gone,
              and all the Doolys, too,
The Mcriartys, and the Dunns,
              and Mrs. old MacHugh ;
The Dalys and Fitzpatricks, with all their kin, and kinds,
Have mounted crumpled papers, on all their window blinds.
Ah ! stop that old piano, you ding it all the day,
It's only when your pupils are here, you make it pay ;
And all your pupils' parents, and all their kin, and kinds,
Have all got crumpled papers, on all their cotton blinds."
He stopped the old piano, and " Vot of zat ? " said he,
" Regarding which, we'll have to do exact the same," said
    she.
" For if we don't, we'll be the talk for many a day to come,
That when all others went abroad, the Zazels kept at home."
It's positively foolish, affects your daughter's hopes—
" Vel, zhere," said he, " go pack ze thronk, I'll tie it vit ze
    ropes ;

And you discharge ze servong, ze moment zat you find,
She's pinned ze crumpled papers, on all ze cotton blind :
And put ze gossip on her tongue, for Switzerland ve sail,
Ze-morrow in ze Dover boat, vot brings ze voreign mail ;
And say, its Oh, so secret, by shings, but she vill blow
Ze news, around ze town, until ze all ze people know."

    ✻   ✻   ✻   ✻   ✻   ✻

The Dover boat had started,
    when, lo ! prospecting round,
A man upon the windows,
    those crumpled papers found.

" Hello ! " said he, " such houses are always left for me,"
And crept into the fanlight, and foraged round with glee.
He stole away the silver, he stole away the clocks,
He augured out the secret, of the children's savings' box ;
He laughed, and he did chuckle, and cackling " Ha ! " said he,
The men who leave their houses thus, are men who toil for me."
Alas ! that in my ballads, I have to tune my song,
To many flats, and minors, to show where sharps go wrong.

He donned a suit,
        next morning,
And sought an auctioneer—
" I'm ordered out to China,
    so harken, and look here ;
Bring up your ivory hammer
    to the house, where you will see,
The blinds in crumpled papers, and cant the lot for me."

He auctioned off the carpets, the suites of every room,
He canted to a builder, the villa for its doom ;
He made him sign a docket, to take down every brick,
Within the shortest notice, so he commenced it quick.
They first upset the chimneys, and then unstitched the slates,
They lifted off the rafters, and rooted out the grates ;
The door, and window casings, they took in several hauls,
And carted off, the debris of bricks, that made the walls.

At length a workman picking
   with crowbar, in the rear,
Let fall his pipe in terror,
   his knees went loose with fear,
A chill of woe electric,
   begirt his heart, like lead,
He found a row of corpses,
   and every corpse was dead !

I've sketched him, with the crowbar, and falling pipe, to show
His awful fright, and sorrow, the fact is, such a blow
Might paralize his senses, unfit him for his trade—
I hope some kindly ladies, will have collections made.
But yet a glamoured beauty was on them all, so nice,
He felt like pins and needles, in glass of strawberry ice,
He shambled round a corner, " O Constable ! " he said,
" I've found a row of corpses, and every corpse is dead ! "
I like that honest fellow, tho' poor, with eye forlorn,
Said he, " O Mister Pleeceman, I wish I wasn't born "—
I've sought again to sketch him, above their ghastly rest,
He indicates a label, on every corpse's breast.

'Twas down an empty cellar,
below the bottle shelves,
They looked as they
were sleeping,
in fact, they
looked
themselves,

The daughters
of Herr Zazel,
the wife of Zazel, and

The Pleeceman asked for Zazel, was he in Switzerland ?
The oldest native, answered a deputating clutch
Of specials, that there never before did happen such,
And so they wrote sensations, and from the civic band,
A posse of detectives, went scoot for Switzerland.

The crowner's Morgue
was opened,
the jurymen were caught,
And every man protested,
although he didn't ought,
They went to view
the corpses.

' Mein gott, vots them ? " said one,
" Votever has there happened, vots been, and gone, and done ?
I could'nt spare ze money, avay mit me, so many,
And so tinks I, I'll mesmer zem all, I vont brings any,
I wraps 'em up mit labels, vots tied upon zem zare,
Ven I comes home, to vake 'em, and sorts 'em up mit care.

I vos in my purse, only ze cash enough to stand,
For vot you calls, von single man, avay in Svitzerland.
And so I mesmerised my vife, my daughters, von by von,
And now I'll vake 'em all, and zen, by shings, you zee me
　　run ! "

He party pumped his arms, he made a maze of passes,
With flashing eyes of flame, that lit his pinc nez glasses.
He clawed with his phalanges as he were going to seize
Some hidden ghost, when lo! at length, his wife began to sneeze,

His wife commenced the sneezing, the girls took up the que,
" Now zee me run, or you vill find, too moosh vor me to do,"
He cried, and off he started, and took the tram for home,
When peering thro' the twilight, of autumn's evening gloam,
He saw a shocking poster, that curdled up his blood,
" This ground to let for building," on which his house had
　　stood,
He laughed a weird, and woful, idiotic laugh at fate,
He took a second tram-car, and sought a barber straight,
And sitting down, he uttered a low despairing groan,
" I'm vot you calls vor Bedlam, so shaves me to ze bone !!"

JOY! ON SEEING A FLYING SPRING.

I MADE him quite at home,
In a villa just by Rome,—
    An Italian, of the antient noble style,—
But I saw him 'neath a star,
And the tink of his guitar,
    Was an irritating thing, that made me smile,
    His object, was my spouse for to beguile,
But when he caught it hot,
With sporting gun, and shot,
He took a flying spring, across a stile !
His object, was my spouse for to beguile.

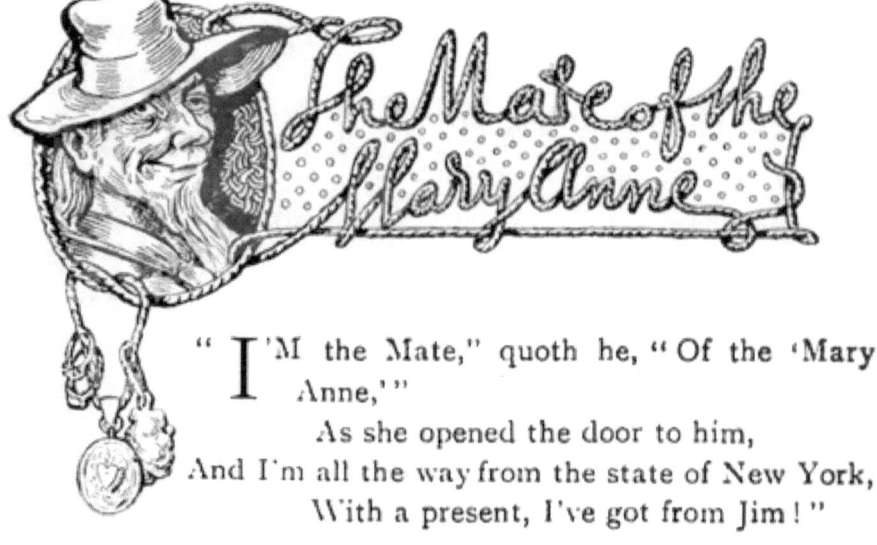

"I'M the Mate," quoth he, "Of the 'Mary
Anne,'"
      As she opened the door to him,
And I'm all the way from the state of New York,
      With a present, I've got from Jim!"

"O dear!" said she, "It's a pleasure to see
      A friend, who has known my son,
We've a party. enjoying the evening tea,
      And you're just in time for fun."

"Ah! thank you," said he, "I would like to explain,
      The chest, is a cumbersome weight,
I'd have brought it myself; but I hadn't the dimes,
      To cover the cost of the freight.

"It's a matter of seventeen shillings and six,
      But you see, I am one of the crew,
I'd have paid it myself, for sake of your son,
      If I could have lifted my screw."

" Ah ! Jim was the very best pal that I knew,"
          She got out the cash for him,
" Now hang up your hat, and come in to the tea,
          And tell us a lot about Jim."

He hung up his hat, and went in to the tea,
          Said he to a girl, who was there,
" You're the livin' dead image of my chum Jim,
          Regardin' yer figure, and hair."

Said he to another, " Yer like yer mother,
          But still the expression of Jim,
Is a playin' around yer beautiful smile,
          A perfeck sister of him.

" I guess you are soft, on the ring that I wear,"
          And he 'splayed his horney fist,
" I'd like you to wear it, for honor of Jim,
          'Twould almost bangle your wrist !

" For savin' his wife, from a shark, I got
          The trinket, at Scooperaboo,
From a Monarch, who gave it me, out of his nose,
          I'm proud to present it to you.

" The ring is too grand, for my tanned hand,
          It's a valuable old gew gaw,
I'm skeered, I'd be robbed o' the thing some night,
          In the grip of a lawless claw.

" It's a putty gay keepsake, that you've got there,
           I'd be glad for sake of poor Jim—"
And he paused, " O yes you may have it," said she,
           " Ah! thanks! when I'm back with him.

" I guess he'll be proud to see it, and hear,
           That I have presented to you,
The ring that I got, for savin' the wife,
           Of the Monarch of Scooperaboo.

" I've a bauble that's here, on a link of my chain,
           It's made of a nugget I got,
I never can know it, I'll maybe be darned!
           Or drowned! or skivered! or shot!

" It's a nugget to waste, with a fellow like me,
           To be sportin' it out of the shop,
Here! take it by gum! you're the mother of Jim!
           Or maybe I'd put it in pop."

" Ah! Sir " said the mother " You're far too kind!"
           As he fastened it on to her chain,
" Will you keep this locket in place of it? there,
           I will never require it again,"

" Aha!" said he. " It's a moral, to see
           You're the spirit of Jim all out,
I'll have it, and wear it, for honour of Jim,
           Without no manner of doubt.

"Eh! what's the time, I am bound to an hour,
        I'd like to remain, if I can,
But the captain's keepin' the cable taut,
        On the men of the ' Mary Anne.'

" Let somebody travel with me to-night,
        Who will carry the luggage ashore,
I'll bring all your compliments out to Jim,
        If I may not see you no more."

Said a girl, who was there, with auburn hair,
        Who hadn't been talking free,
" The weather is dark, and you say the ship,
        Is out some yards at sea,

" It's better that two, should travel with you,
        The journey's a little too far,
And one'll take charge of the present from Jim,
        The other, can go for a car."

So two of the gentlemen, offered to go,
        Who had been at the evening tea,
And they all shook hands, and the three took tramp,
        To the wall, by the wailing sea.

" I guess that we ought to be havin' a quench,"
        Said the Mate, " For I always do,
I never go thirsty, aboard at night,"
        So he went, and treated the two.
                     G

They sat in a room, at the back of the bar,
   Discussing three tumblers hot,
" I'm darned, if we won't have a couple of smokes ! "
   Said he, " And I'll settle the shot."

" You'll pull a cigar with me, by gum !
   I'll get them ' and jest you set,' "
He went with his purse, to the bar to pay,
   And they have not seen him yet !

But whether he's shot, or whether he's drowned,
   Or darned, the Host did say,
Behind the bar, as he pulled a pint,
   That " the drink was still to pay ! "

      *   *   *   *

She laughed a laugh, when the twain returned,
   " You're a mighty discerning pair ! "
And she posed her nose, with a tilted tip,
   Did the girl, with the auburn hair.

They all suggested, a different way,
   Of finding the missing Mate,
" Put out your brains," said the auburn hair,
   " On a clean, blue pattern plate.

" And twig a few of the cobwebs off,
   From Scooperaboo, look there !
We've Brumagem trinkets, of glass, and brass ! "
   Said the girl, of the auburn hair.

AN UMBRELLA CASE.

I saw a dress! 'twas of my wife,
She stepped along with frivol rife,
And by her side, a man of strife
          A guardsman of the line.

Ha ha! So ho! was here a cause,
To agitate the Probate laws,
For a divorce, I did not pause,
          With guardsman of the line,

I had an umbrella stout,
I lifted it, I flung it out,
In semicircle, with a shout,
          At guardsman of the line!

Ah! me, for an unlucky wight!
Beneath the sick electric light,
She turned, O shock unto my sight!
          She was no wife of mine!

He didn't draw, I wasn't slain,
But of that blow, he did complain,
And made me wipe away the stain,
          With legal brief, and twine.

A Story

TOLD BY

JONES

ONE evening, as in troubled mood,
     I sampled Rotten Row,
Across my scapula, I got
     A sharp conclusive blow !

A flat concussion of a palm,
      Was quick, and deftly laid,
With rude familiar frowardness,
      Against my shoulder blade !
The impact curled up my blood ;
      And almost in a thrice,
My heart refrigerated, to
      An imprompt lump of ice !

I feared it was a bailiff, and
      I sprang from off the sod !
" I'm but a ghost ! " said he, " you need
      Not start " said I " thank God !
" I must confess, that I eschew
      A bailiff's companie,
" A ghost, is much more welcome, to
      A person fixed like me."

Thus into swift acquaintanship,
      Familiarly did glide,
The spook of Rotten Row, and I,
      And walking side by side,
We chatted in a varied way,
      And slowly sauntered round,
Until we came upon a lone,
      And sparsy plot of ground,

Then halting there, the spectre cried,
      In accents like a knell,
" T'was here I fought a duel once,
      And there it was I fell !
Behold a thistle growing there,

And yon a shamrock too,
And there in every season past,
A little wild rose grew,
A nursery in miniature,
Of sign of Kingdoms three,
That sprang spontaneous thro' the sod,
From blood, that flowed from me,
For lo! my sire was Rupert Smith,
My mater was a Lynch;
My grandmother per pater, was
A Flora Jane Mac Tinch,
An uncle, on the mother's side,
A Belfast Macinfee,
This made the union perfect,
And embodied thus in me,
Was typed the British Empire,
Per my consanguinitee.
And it's an interesting fact,
That Wales can share the fame,
And pride, of my nativity,
For, Jones, it was the name,
My mother first accepted, as
A matrimonial claim ;
But Jones was testily inclined,
And all about a myth,
In jealous hate, he fell before
The blade, of Rupert Smith !
Then Rupert Smith, he minded of
The widow's wail, and tear,
And in remorse, he married her,
As consequence, I'm here !

The record of my gallant sire,
      To hot complexion grew,
In me, till I was minded of
      A cause, for fighting too.
I knew a maid, and for her sake,
      My daily life was fuss,
It is not always for a maid,
      A man's affected thus ;
But when she wasn't by my side,
      I felt how lonely, space
Would be, if man could not behold,
      A single woman's face.
And so I fondled, petted her,
      And worried, wrote some rhymes,
And even got them published, in
      A small, suburban times,
I took some pestilential pains,
      To learn the minuet,
And trained my voice, to harmonise,
      With her's, in the duet.

We married were, I faith ! it was
      A festal day, for hope,
To care we gave the congè, and
      To pleasure, extra scope,
Until one day, my joy was washed
      Away, like scented soap !
'Twas on this wise,—
        In Rotten Row,
      Midst fashionable life,
I found a promenader there,
      In converse, with my wife !
I parleyed not a moment, but
      Asserting manhood's law,

I tweaked him by the nose, and cried,
      " Defend thyself and draw ! "
Resenting my impetuous way,
      The old command, to teach,
He roused him to impromptu fire,
      Of indignation speech,
And with a sneer, that galled my quick,
      He swore me, I must die !
But with a rough right royal oath,

I sneered him back the lie !
" Thy name ? " quoth I, " I am," said he,
        " A man of Deeds, and Loans,
                And auction sales,
                I come from Wales,
        My name is Mervyn Jones ! "
" What ?
        Mervyn Jones of Pontypridd ? "
        " Exactly so, the same,"
Said he,—I heard of him before,
        And quivered at his name !
For 'twas the name, thro' which the world
        Had come to hear of me,
By pruning blade of Smith, on Jones ;
        His genealogic tree,
" Yes I am Jones ! "
Quoth he, " By loans,
        And mortgaged, for her life,
Thro' debts to me, attorney's power,
        I hold upon thy wife,
So skin thy blade, I'll give thee cause,
        To tweak my nose ! " he saith,
" I'll auction thee, unto the bid,
        Of good old broker death ! "—
Hereditary fate it seemed,
        That I must fight with Jones,
I would have shirked it, but for those,
        His irritating tones,
I feared a compensating fate,
        Might strike an even deal,
Betwixt the house of Smith, and Jones,

But skinning forth my steel,
I smote at him, by hip, and thigh,
      By carte, and aye by tierce,
I held him to his guard, with quick,
      Aggressive strokes, and fierce,
But lo! the cunning of my wrist,
      A moment lapsed! with art
Of subtle fencer, past my guard,
      He pinked me, in the heart!
It skivered me, just like the fork,
      That spoils a grilling steak,
I shivered, with a yell, and then,
      A woman's cry,—and crake
Of joy from him, with mighty pang,
      I leaped in air, and fell!
A muffled music thrilled my brain;
      For me, the passing knell,
From numbing toe, and finger tip,
      The graduating thrill
Of life's collapse, crept over me,
      I wriggled, and lay still!
Then, from the chrysolid of flesh,
      Light spirited I rose,
And gazed upon my corse, as on
      A suit of cast off clothes,
My widow shrieked, and fainted, but
      A golden vinagarette,
My slayer lifted from his fob,
      And to her nose, he set
The bauble, while he pinched her, slapped
      Her hands, and brought her to,

Then speaking to my mortal wreck,
      Said he, " Now as for you,
I have avenged the slur upon
      My nose, thy tweak hath wrought,
Thou art the loser, in the game
      Of combat, that thou sought,
But lo! thy widow, will not weep
      It long, for I may say,
She'll shed her weeds, and she will wed
      With me, the first of May!
Then, with my spouse upon his arm,
      He turned, and sneaked away,
And left me here, a widowed ghost,
      Aye, even to this day! "
My indignation at his wrongs,
      I told the grateful spook :
" Gramercy! " cried he, as with misty
      Fist, my hand he shook,
And charged me thus, with eager verve,
      Of deep revengeful tones,
" If ever thou dost meet a man,
      Who deals in deeds, and loans,
Who bears the patronymic, and
      The shield, of Mervyn Jones,
I care not how, by forgery!
      By fist, or aye by knife !
By sneaking of his fiancée,
      Or mayhap of his wife !
By burgling of his premises,
      Or pelting him with stones !
Avenge me, on the offspring, of

The man, called Mervyn Jones!"
I sware him, if such christened man,
    Did ever dare my sight,
In widest open day, or from
    The nooks, of darkest night!
It mattered not, if extra tall,
    Or what his weight, or width,
I'd borrow from him, to avenge
    The wrongs, of Rupert Smith!
" I thank thee well!" the spectre cried,
    With chuckle, sad, and grim,
" Adieu!"
        And lo! he vanished thro'
    The hazy gloaming dim:
He vanished, and I thanked my luck,
    He left no aching bones!
For I'm a male descendant, of
    The man, called Mervyn Jones!
And Mervyn, haps my christian name,
    A broker, I am he,
A windfall fructifaction, of
    That genealogic tree.

                ⁂   ⁂

Next evening, when I told this tale,
    To Doctor Bolus Chuff,
Incredulous, and unimpressed,
    With mien, erect, and tough,
Presenting a prescription, for
    Some tonic tempered pills,
Said he " Thro' too much spirits, you
    Have got D.T.'s and chills!"

THE MAGIC SPECS

HE WROUGHT a specs, with magic rim, of strange, and subtle parts,
For by those optics made by him, he saw men's inmost hearts,
The grim old sage, 'twas of his fads, to wear those wrysome lamps,
For evermore, and find the lads, the worldly-wise, and scamps.

He saw the plottings, and the strife, he saw the woes, and tears !
The murky glooms of unknown life, the spring of hopes, and fears,
The sham of face, the sham of name, the sham of heart within ;
He sifted all, and wrote for fame, record of unknown sin.

" Ho, ho ! " cried he at length, " I wis, the dross of men is such,
'Tis surfeit, thus to seek for this, it palls me overmuch ;
I'll seek a gem of human hearts, and find it, if I can,"—
He sought at home, and foreign parts, to meet an honest man.

In that pursuit, a year and seven, did on his labours fall ;
" Heigho ! " cried he, " outside of Heaven, they're masks, and faces all !

They're masks, and faces all!" quoth he, and from the world
    he went
To bide alone, beside the sea, in selfish self-content.

Now, this old sage, thro' many a year, had never thought of self,
Before he used the specs: in fear, his mirror, on a shelf,
He set, with face down evermore, lest by a glance, that he
Should pry into the evil store, of his own villainie.

But, fishing in a pool one day, the sage forgot his specs—
To take it from his nose,—and hey! a horror, to perplex
His soul with fear, was under him; for, in the glassy wave,
He saw his heart reflected grim! he saw his new-made grave:

He saw, that he himself was worst, of all that he had seen;
By sight of conscience, he was curst, the evil deeds, had been
Dry rotting in his blackened heart, the place he feared to search,
And self-reproach, did send a dart, that knocked him off his
    perch;
The rod and line, fell from his hand, the specs fell off his nose:
And he was drowned, in sight of land, in all his Sunday clothes.

Ye Curious Tayle of ye Uncivil Fight of ye Civil Warre

ODDZOOKS! ye civil war was rough,
'Twixt cavalier, and roundhead tough,
Thence, for thy pale
Of cheek, and wail,
Now hearken, to ye curious tayle,

Ah! me.

THEY met, to meet, was cause for strife
And hunger, for each other's life!
Alack ah! me,
That such should be,
Where posies, pied beneath ye tree,

Ah! me.

IN derring do, they straightway play,
  And cut, and slash, ye time away;

Ye evil grue,

This derring do,

When earth, was wide enough for two,

Ah! me.

L O! one at length, in bonds did pine,
    Ye squirrel came, and nipped ye twine;
        Reproof of spite,
        From woodland mite,
For truce to-ye fanatic fight,

                    Ah! me.

B UT hey alack ! again they rise,
.s; And swish their blades, in murderous wise ;

’Tis pain, to sing,

Of sword, in swing,

Where butterflies, did spread ye wing,

Ah ! me.

ye Fytte
of ye
Seconde Bout.

AT length, one trussed his foe, but lo!
  A bat, did cut ye cord, ho! ho!
        Ye moral flat,
        Of gracious bat,
That men, should drop ye hate, like that—

                    Ah! me.

Y E wrath of wrong, is still to do,

    Ye loathsome vengeance, starts anew,

        O pity ! wrong,

        Should wreak so strong,

Where birds, did pipe ye ev'ensong,

           Ah ! me.

Ye Nervous Trytte.

YE strife waxed hot, in air they spring,—
No fiercer fray, did minstrel sing,—
But why spill here,
Ye tender tear,
For Roundhead, or ye Cavalier?

Ah! me.

Ye Fytte of Ye
Timely Sting.

Yͤ Fytte
of yͤ Discovery

THEY scuffle, till each wig, and nose,
Fell off, and nature's truths, disclose,

Ye wild surprise,

Doth swiftly rise,

Ye brows, above ye startled eyes!

Ah! me.

FOR lo ! they recognise each one,

Each was his father's other son !

Ye clasping spree,

Of filial glee,

Is here depicted, as you see,

Ah ! me.

Ye Fraternal Fytte.

Leather Versus

AN instance of calculating foresight and prudence is illustrated in the following verses. If men would rely on the mutual study of a spirit of equity, and enter more confidentially into the claims of each, what beautiful pictures, of repentant resignation to a just castigation, would be afforded, by certain of those who misunderstand the rights of property. An excellent lesson of this kind, is taught by the experience of the first tramp. He parted from the Farmer, with comprehensive impressions, of the farmer's energy, and application to business, a fact, which he took the earliest opportunity, of advertising in the nearest hospital. Thro' the second case, also runs a beautiful lesson, to the farmer, it may not have happed so well, as to the tramp, but the record serves to show, that an action at law, should only result, as a mutual alternative, agreeable to both parties; thereby the air of the Law Courts, would be considerably purified, of the stuffiness, that oppresses the impetuous litigant.

SAID one tramp, to the
    second tramp,
"The dark is comin' on
    the sun,
Do you prowl in to this 'ere
    barn,
    And I'll dodge on to
        yonder one.

" I allus likes to sleep alone,
          Besides you see, it runs' em tight,
The Varmers, when a pair o' tramps
          Turns up, so Bill, I'll say good night."

The chanticleer, did early trump,
          A tonic note, upon his pipe,
And woke the husbandman, to view,
          How thick, and tall, his crops, and ripe.

And in his barn, he found a tramp !
          " Ho, trespasser, what shall I do ? "
He cried " Shall I evict by Law ?
          Or take the Law myself, on you ? "

" Well Varmer, I have had with cranks,
          Of legal jaw, too much," said he,
" So with your leave, I'd rather you,
          Would take the law, yourself on me."

" Ha ! that's exactly to my form ! "
          He gripped him by the neck, " Here goes !
Whew ! now take this ! and that, and this,"
          With that, he gave him all his toes.

He kicked him, thro' the barn door,
          He rolled him, in the grunty stye,
And up, and down, and round the yard,
          And then, he bunged him in the eye !

He ducked him, in the horses' pond,
      He slung him, right across a load
Of dung, he kicked him thro' the gate,
      And wiped him up and down the road!

He kicked him black! He kicked him blue!
      He kicked him green! and red and white!
He kicked him, till he could not kick,
      For then the tramp was out of sight!

That tramp did never more appear
      Around that neighbourhood,
        he passed
Away, just like a whiff of smoke,
      That scuds before the autumn
        blast!

    *   *   *   *

A second husbandman that morn,
      Was quick astir, he fancied he
Did hear, a wailing in his barn,
      A moan, as of the wild banshee!

He thought to catch the female sprite,
      For truth, he was a festive scamp,
But got a sort of snub, when he,
      Discovered but a snoring tramp!

The sleep was deep, for with his foot,
          He had to supplement the blow,
Or box, he gave him on his ear,
          And shouted in that ear " Hello !

You'll pardon me, my friend, but 'ere,
          I thought, this barn belonged to me !
Now shall I chuck you out myself,
          Or seek injunct, from Chancerie ? "

The startled tramp, did rub his nose,
          And stared that farmer, in the eye,
Then stretched himself, and spoke as he,
          Would fain enjoy a longer lie.

" Well Boss, I've been so often chucked,
          That it would be relief to stay,
And in the Court of Chancerie,
          Arrange it in a friendly way."

They took the case to chancerie,
          And argued it, from every point,
But in the end, they always found,
          The arguments, were out of joint !

The prosecuting counsel, cranked
          The cogs of all the tramp's defence,
And also in his turn, was spanked,
          And thus, they cribbed the farmer's pence.

They argued it, on every side,
        With judge's whim, and lawyer's yarn,
But still the tramp, remains at home,
        His home, is in the farmer's barn !

The case, has not been ended yet,
        It crops up now, and often then,
You cannot tell, when it may crop,
        It might crop up, next week again,

But when that tramp, will have to go,
        I cannot tell it, nor can he,
The farmer cannot, nor can they ;
        The lawyers of the Chancerie.

Thus tho' we may not take the law,
        Into our hands, it's often meet,
To serve extemporaneous writ
        By sharp eviction, from the feet.

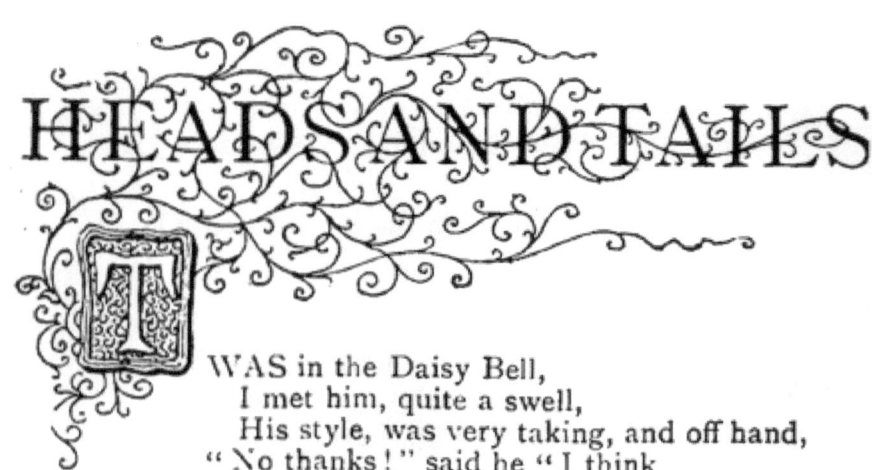

HEADS AND TAILS

'T WAS in the Daisy Bell,
 I met him, quite a swell,
  His style, was very taking, and off hand,
   " No thanks!" said he " I think
We'll toss up, for the drink,
  I'm independent, as there's in the land!"

I tossed him, and I lost,
Said he " That was a frost,
  I'll toss you now, a consolation toss,
I'll toss you, for a bob"
I lost! " I wouldn't rob"
  Said he " I wouldn't see you, at a loss.

" By gum! here's what I'll do,
I'll toss you now for two,
  It's double now, or quits, that we will try,"
Again I lost: 'twas queer,
Again, said he. " look here,
  Your fortune, will be lifting by and by."

I thought that it must turn,
But soon I had to learn,
  His way was rather taking, and off hand,
A goodly sum was due,
Said he " I've made off you,
  Six quid, and sixteen tanners, you will stand,"
" Your double coin," said I,
" Has just now caught my eye,
  And the dust, from your jacket, I must whack!"
  His jacket, with malacca, I did crack!
  His hide, was very taking, at the back!

The Colonel and the Cook

"OH COLONEL I could love you,
    With faithful heart," said she;
"But you are far too noble—
    Too grand a man for me,
For you're Commander of the Horse,
    And hardly could be higher,
While, I am only just a Cook,
    Around the kitchen fire."

Said she "I could not marry you,
    For you are all so grand;
I'd be a most unhappy wife—
    The saddest in the land."
Said he, "I did not ask you;
    But when I'm far from you,
And on the field of battle,
    I'll see what I can do."

Said he, " I never thought of it,
        And only now, I see—
Perhaps you are the woman,
        Would suit to wed with me,
And that is just the cause of them—
        The words, I said to you—
When on the field of battle,
        I'll see what I can do."

The town, was all in tumult
        Of women's wail alack!
For many a gallant soldier,
        Would never more come back,
And even he (the Colonel)
        Might fall—the first or last ;
And that's the chiefest reason,
        That Cook was weeping fast.

And tho' it was not proper,
    To see the Colonel, look
With visage of dejection,
    Upon a humble cook,
Yet nature won't be cheated,
    Despite of high degree.
" Adieu ; I'll come back worthy,
    My love, to wed with thee."
And that is how they parted,
    And those, the words he said :
And oft, when she was cooking,
    It came into her head,
The promise he had uttered,
    Of sweetest memory—
" Adieu ; I'll come back worthy,
    My love, to wed with thee."

She took a thought one morning,
    And bought a copy-book ;
Said she, I'll study pothooks,

They're suited for a cook.
I'll write his name, in roundhand,
A letter, I will send,
With the words "no more at present"—
My pet name, at the end.

She wrote his name, in roundhand,
A letter, she did send,
With " No more now at present,"
Her pet name, at the end.
But it never, never reached him,
And he did languish yet,
For the Cook, at home in Erin
He never could forget.

But lo ! a taste for learning,
Is like a taste for drink,
While working on the pothooks,
She then began to think.
And thought, is like a snowball,
That gathers every turn ;
She studied read-'em-easys,
While joints began to burn.

She studied, night and morning,
At languages, and paint,
At poetry, and musty prose,
And legends, old, and quaint.
She wrote a three-vol. novel,
And got a fancy price,
Became a photo beauty ;
" Oh, this," quoth she, "is nice ! "

She then appeared in drama,
    While posing there, with grace
Of gauze, and limelight glowing
    Upon her lovely face;
A common soldier, shouted
    From the Olympian rail—
"O 'evans!" its my 'Arriet,
    And turning deadly pale.

He darted for the stage door,
Her carriage grand, was there,
She was about to enter,
With all the fuss, and flare,
Of mashers buzzing round her;
And plunging forth, said he—
" I'm wot was once a Colonel, who went across the sea.
    " Of course you must remember,
        The words, I said to you—
    ' When on the field of battle,
        I'd see what I could do.'
    I never make a promise,
        But to my word, I stick.
    The man, who breaks his promise,
        Is but a broken brick."

I'm wot was once a Colonel,
    And for your love, I strove,
To be reduced, into the ranks,
    For sake of you, my love;
I ran away in battle, I several times got drunk,
Was challenged to a duel, and purposely took funk.
They whittled my commission, into a major's rank,
And still I acted badly, and several times I drank,
I managed to get nibbled, down to a sergeant then
I stole a pint of whiskey, was put amongst the men.

"I've been all over
    Europe,
A lookin' out for you,
I have eschewed my
    grammar,
To prove my 'eart,
    was true;
I've parted with my
    surname,
That all might well
    combine,

Which now, I'm Private Miggins, of the Seventy-seventh Line.
    "I've got a vulgar accent,
        And vulgar sayin's too.
    I drink, from common pewter.
        It's all along of you,
    And generally, my manners,
        Are much about the styles,
    You'll find amongst the manners,
        Of the people of St. Giles.

" But here, I say, look, listen !
    You have not acted straight,
But made us yet the victims,
    Of a lobsided fate ;
While I've been levellin' downwards,
    To suit with your degree,
You've been, and gone, and levelled up,
    Contrarywise to me.

" You had not ought to take me,
    So short as this, I say ;
You've worked a mean advantage,
    While I was far away.
But still, we'll go to-morrow,
    And make our love complete."
" Get out ! " she cried, and vanished,
    In her brougham, down the street.

HE was one of the middle age
        men I wot,
A troubadour bedight,
Who lost himself, in a lonely wood,
    An exceptional sort of night,
        For the moon, was only beginning to wax,
            And the clouds, were muggy, and black,
    And there wasn't much chance, of finding his way,
            To the trail, of the beaten track.

But troubadours, were stout and strong,
        Of tough, and stubborn, stuff,
    And took the rough, with the sleek, and smooth,
        The smooth, with the rusty rough,
    So up thro' the drift, of the hummocky ruck,
            Of the clouds, he searched for a star,
    To serenade, with the thringumy-thrang,
            Of the thrum, of his new guitar.

The glint of one, thro' a galloping cloud,
      He caught, and he screwed his wire,
And gave a twist, to its patent head,
      And toned the catgut higher.
Then flung the cape of his cloak aside,
      And in an æsthetic strain,
He pitched his voice, to the concert key,
      And twanged on the strings amain.

But having expressed
   himself in song,
With a quivering
     verse or two,
His favourite string
   gave out, with a bang,
   And stopped
     his impromptu.

He muttered a satire upon that string,
      And sat on a bank, close by,
When he heard the trip of a female foot,
      And lisp of a female sigh!

She was one of the guardians, of the piece
      Of ground, that was round him there,
An ariel spirit in azure blue,
      And fluffs of auburn hair,
That framed a very attractive face,
      Of cream, and strawberry pink,
And she greeted the troubadour bedight,
      With a captivating wink!

" O troubadour, what brings you here,
      So lone and sad ? " said she,
Just throw your guitar across your back,
      And wander away with me.
I'll show you the fairy dells, of mine,
      All tricked around with sheen,
Of glittering gold, and sparkling gems,
      With electric lights between.

" I'm a single woman, and never was
      once
In love, with a man,
      till this ! "
And then she stooped
   to his quivering lip,
Imprinting a dainty kiss.
" Why don't you get up
   out of that ? " she cried,
And make no longer stay,
But a spirit within, still
   held him down,
In a magical sort of way.

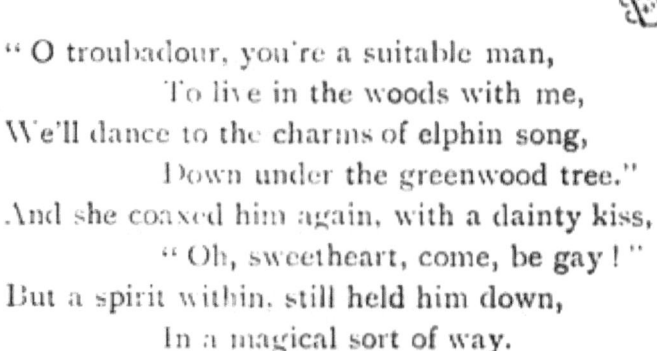

" O troubadour, you're a suitable man,
      To live in the woods with me,
We'll dance to the charms of elphin song,
      Down under the greenwood tree."
And she coaxed him again, with a dainty kiss,
      " Oh, sweetheart, come, be gay ! "
But a spirit within, still held him down,
      In a magical sort of way.

"I hope, that you don't imagine," said she,
   "That I am a frivolous flirt,
I'm the woman, that's new, the fashion to-day,
  With rational trunks, for skirt,
I can ride, on a bicycle, made for two,
   Or 'tec out the sins of town,"
But all he could do, was give her a grin,
   From the spirit that held him down !

He'd have given the world, to get up out of that,
   But a tantalising sprite,
Had taken possession of him, you see,
   In the early part of the night.
The fact of it is, that he couldn't get up,
   If she gave him a kingly crown,
And all he could do, was give her a grin,
   From the spirit, that held him down !

Twas woe ! to see an attractive maid,
   So slurred, by a knightly bard,
A misery this, for her plaint of love,
   To be grinned at, snubbed, and marred !
Yet ever again, did she give him a kiss,
   And a lingering, coaxing smile,
But the spirit within, still held him down,
   In a magical sort of style !

"O come get up out of that !" she cried,
   And gave his collar a shake,
With a kick in the ribs, that bustled him up,
   And startled him wide awake!
And her raiment shrunk to the belted blue,

Of a burly man, said he,
"Yer out very late, in a dress like that,
So track it along with me."
" Get up out of that," the constable cried,
" And don't make no delay,"
But the spirit within, still held him down,
In a magical sort of way.
The spirit within, still held him down,
But the constable bent his back,
And hooshed him up, and carried him off,
At once to the beaten track.

The troubadour, came into the dock
Next day, in a crowded court,
And the rig of his garb, to the modern herd,
Was a source of evil sport.
But the modern beak had no romance,
And the sum of a couple of crown,
He fined the unfortunate troubadour,
For the spirit that held him down !

HIS FUTURE STATE.

I FOUND him, sitting on a seat,
     With sad reflective mien,
A drowsing pathos, in his eye,
     Tinged with a tint of green,
I sat him by " good friend " I said,
     " Of pilgrims, the resort,
Is this a church ? " I wish it wor ! "
     Cried he, " It's Bow Street Court ! "

And then again, I looked at him,
     Once more, I spoke him kind,
" Thy far off gaze, doth indicate,
     Some presence, on thy mind,
Some haunting thought,
     of grave import,
     Connected with the fate,
Perchance, that thou,
     mayhap, may meet,
     When in the future state.
O speak the burden of thy heart,
     That I may note it down,"

" It be's I was a boozin', and
     I'm fined a quid and crown,
My far off look, is for that fine,
     To dodge the prison gate,
And warders' lock on fourteen days,
     That quads my future state.

A MOST attractive lady, of middle class degree,
When in the Ranelagh Gardens, was thus addressed, as she
Beheld a man, she jilted, " Theresa Mary Jane,
You didn't think to see me back in town, so soon again ;
It's most exasperating, that when my back I turn
You pace the Ranelagh Gardens, with cotton-ball O'Byrne."
The linen draper started, and with indignant shout,
Said he. " She loves me only, you ferule-fingered lout,
Your time you're only wasting, so take a thought, and spurn,
The idle hopes. that lure ye," said Mister Pat O'Byrne.

Just then up came a stranger, with bending courtesy,
He doffed his triple tilted. " Good-night, mam'selle," said he,

Then turning to O'Gorman, and then, to Pat O'Byrne,
" Ze manners of ze shentlemans, ze both of you should learn ;
To wrangle round ze lady, I'm shames of you, by dam !
If ye don't know ze fencin' of ze duel, go, and cram,
Don't bring ze crowds around her, but mit ze mornin' lark,
Vash out in blood, ze quarrels all in ze Phœnix Park."
" I'm on," said Kit O'Gorman. " Begor, an' so am I,"
Said Pat O'Byrne. The lady, then gave a tender sigh,
She told them each, she loved him, and though her heart did
    bleed,
Expressed a wish, he'd combat on a small Arabian steed.
" The duel's getting prosy, invest it with a fling
Of tournamental glory, you'll find it's now the thing,
To gild, with knightly glamour, your daring feat of strife,
And he who kills the other, I'll be his wedded wife ;
Till then I'm Queen of beauty," so spake that lady fair,
" I give you both a fortnight, that each may well prepare,
And then I'll send you chargers, on which to combat so "
(Her father dealt in horses), " now, sirs, good-night, and go."
The fix was fraught with danger, for each of those two men,
Existence is too precious, man can't be born again ;
They ne'er had used a weapon, they never strode a horse,
It was extremely awkward, and couldn't well be worse.
So while O'Gorman practised with foil, and mask, O'Byrne,
Was in a circus riding, and then he took his turn,
Before a fencing-master, to guard, and thrust, and fool,
While Pat O'Gorman, cantered around a riding school.
At length the fencing-master, he says to Pat O'Byrne,
" You're perfect mit ze fencing, you've nodings more to learn."
The man who taught him riding, did compliment him too,
And Kit O'Gorman also had " nodings " more to do.

✲   ✳   ✲   ✳   ✲   ✳   ✲

The fortnight was now over, the morning came at last,
The rising dawn, was ushered with snow, and biting blast,
As on the Fifteen Acres, all in the Phœnix Park,
The duellists were waiting the Arab steeds, when, hark!
They heard a distant braying, as 'twere a trump of brass,
'Twas followed by a donkey, and then a second ass,
Came guided by his halter, unto the fated spot,
Said Pat O'Byrne and O'Gorman, "O, powdhers, this is rot!"
But yet a queen of beauty was their's the prize to win.
"We better pause no longer, but instantly pitch in,"
Said Pat O'Byrne, and Gorman. They tossed for choice of ass,
And pick of blade, then wheeling, they faced upon the grass.
I was for Kit O'Gorman a second on that day,
To see the flashing rapiers, to hear the donkeys bray
Was sight and sound to think of, the sylvan haunts were rife
With echoes reverbrated from crash of deadly strife;
Up went each donkey backwards, while scintillating wales
Of flashing steels, were echoed, by lashing of their tails,
For lo! the fight was doubled, the skittish donkeys sought,
To variegate the contest, and capered round, and fought;
They gave no chance. The foemen, with awkward clink of
    steels.
Struck now and then, while skew-ways the donkeys fought
    with heels.
'Twas six o'clock commencing, and now, the strokes of ten,
Were sounding from the city, and still these mounted men,
Had not received abrasion, a cut, a prod, or crack,
When both were somersaulted, from off each asses' back;
The weapons went in splinters, as on the frosty grass,
Each foeman sprawled a moment, and loudly cursed his ass.

The assmen, quickly bounded unto their feet again,
And watched the seconds, chasing the donkeys round the plain;
And when at length, we caught them, and brought them back
    once more,
With fits of indignation, the baffled foemen swore;
"Bad scran to it!" said Gorman, "O'Musha, "yis bad scran"
Cried Pat O'Byrne, "It's not a fight, for any dacent man,
Four mortial hours we've struggled—an' I'm all in a sweat!"
Said Gorman "Pon me sowl, I got no chance to kill ye yet!"
"The fight has been protracted, and divil a thing is done,
I vote we go and tell her, said O'Byrne, "that it's no fun,
To fight, as we've been fighting. Tib's Eve might come, and
    go,
We'd still be found here fooling her donkeys thro' the snow."

       ✢   :   ✢

They felt a queer foreboding of something, going down
Parkgate-street, on that morning, till journeyed back to town;
They sought the girl, to tell her the fix that they were in,
When a larky-looking servant in the hall, began to grin.

"She's not at home at present, but breakfast sure is laid,
She's gone off to be married,' outspoke the sneering maid;
"Le Beau, the fencin'-master is now the blissful man;
You'll see them soon, they're comin' in a satin-lined sedan."

"O, blur-an-owns!" said Gorman, "O tear o'war," said Byrne,
MacHugh, the other second, and I got quite a turn!
The man, who heard them quarrel, in Ranelagh-walk that night,
Was Le Beau, the man who sent them to Phœnix Park to
    fight.

He taught them both in fencing, and yet they did not know,
That each, was being instructed by his rival, Mons. Le Beau.

They tied her pair of donkeys, unto her garden pier,
When from the topmost window, that servant shouted "Here,
A note she left to give you, for both of you to learn."
'Twas written : " Kit O'Gorman, and Mister Pat O'Byrne,
I've sent a couple of donkeys, I thought that they might teach
What fools you are, for fighting, for what's beyond your reach,
But, silly as my donkeys, if both of you remain,
Remorse for death, will follow,
                    I'm yours, Theresa Jane."

We sought a Pub, and pondered, and drank, and sadly swore,
We would not be connected, with duels evermore,
I drank of stout, O'Gorman, and Byrne, of harder stuff,
They swore of duel fooling, they both had quite enough,—
Now, here's the bunch of fives, boys, there is no better rod
To 'venge our wounded honour, than the weapons made by
    God !

THE ABDICATED CROWN.

He WAS jolly, round, and fat,
And with a bright top hat,
    A chain beneath his burly bosom set,
In good old fashioned way,
Said he to me, " I say
    Old boy, I have a thing that's to be met,
        A pressing little debt,
        The dunner has me set,
    My pocket is unfurnished, to be let !
Five bob is all I ask,"
I 'sponded to the task,
    That abdicated crown is debit yet !

K

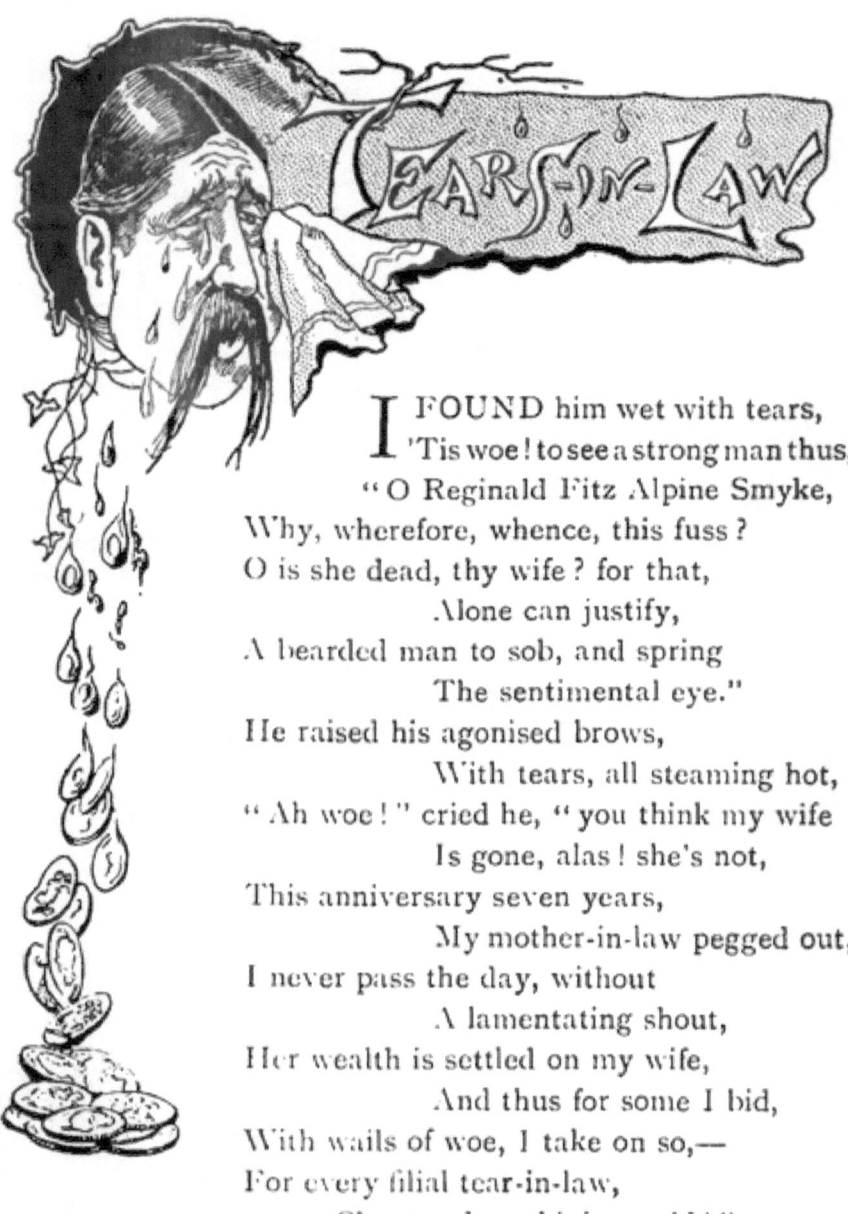

I FOUND him wet with tears,
'Tis woe! to see a strong man thus,
"O Reginald Fitz Alpine Smyke,
Why, wherefore, whence, this fuss?
O is she dead, thy wife? for that,
        Alone can justify,
A bearded man to sob, and spring
        The sentimental eye."
He raised his agonised brows,
        With tears, all steaming hot,
"Ah woe!" cried he, "you think my wife
        Is gone, alas! she's not,
This anniversary seven years,
        My mother-in-law pegged out,
I never pass the day, without
        A lamentating shout,
Her wealth is settled on my wife,
        And thus for some I bid,
With wails of woe, I take on so,—
For every filial tear-in-law,
        She stands a shining quid!"

I left him weeping up the stairs,
       I met his wife below,
" I'll call," said I "another day,
       Your husband takes on so,"
" And so he may take on," she said,
       " His crocodiles may fall,
'Twill drain some water from his brain,
       And do him good, that's all,
To-day in the domestic stocks,
       He'll find a sudden fall!"

Alas! for poor Fitz Alpine Smyke,
       His confidence was meant
For me alone, but she was there,
       In slippers, on the scent!
Then came an action for divorce,
       With all its quips, and cranks,
And *nisi* was the laws *decree*
       That dropped him to the ranks,
And then he sought for many cribs,
       The cribs he did not suit,
But he could well dissimulate,
       So he became a mute,
His wife took the hymeneal bond
       Again, and then she died,
And hired mutes with sorry mien,
       Were by her coffin's side.
But when the funeral was o'er,
       The widower he went
And greeted one of those—the mutes—
       With feeling compliment,

He lightly pinched him by the crape
   "O Mister Mute, I say,
I wish I could have wept the tears,
   That you have dropped to-day!"
"Ah! me alack!" the mute exclaimed,
   " My sorrow was sincere,
And were I not the ass I am,
   We wouldn't both be here;
For I am he, Fitz Alpine Smyke,
   Thro' tears, I let her slip,
And now by tears, I eke it out
   In salary and tip."

HE FOLLOWED THE FOX.

FOLLOWED the fox, tally ho!

I followed the fox, with a go, by Joe!
As swift as a swallow, or crow,
                              Wo ho !

The ditch, is a cropper, hello!
I am in it ! and out, and a show !
Am asked to the next, won't go!

E was a courteous manager—
    a Bosser of the Bank,
He filled the post of Chairman,
    and other seats of rank.
But he was never envied,
    his screw was almost nil—
Ten thousand pounds per annum,
    and chances from the till.

One day, when he was wiping his specks, thought he, " I hold,
I'm working all for nothing by a heap of solid gold.
I'll make of it a custom, a couple of months or so,
To leave the strong room open as in and out I go.
And fitfully in absence of mind, I'll drop my bunch
Of keys about, and leave them when going down for lunch.
The point of which is plainly, that on a certain night,
I'll seize on all the Bullion, and fix it out of sight.
I will not be suspected, I'll do whate'er I please,
For I have clinked the vintage with nobles and M.P.'s ;
And though I know he's honest, I'll make it so appear,
That I will prove the robber, is the honest young cashier.

They'll pass a vote
        of censure,
that I did leave behind,
        My keys,
and strong room open,
  but, pshaw!
     I need not mind.
'Twill come out
        on the trial,
I'll make it sure
       and clear,
'Twas all of too much trust in the honest young cashier."

He left the strong room open; he left his keys about,
Upon his mantle-shelf, and desk, anon when he went out—
A custom not unnoticed by him, the young cashier,
Who got a stick of wax, and what he did with it is clear.

One night there was a darkness, like crape upon the land,
And such a gust and thunder, a man could hardly stand.
The tempest was so fearsome, that if you spoke in shouts,
'Twould only be a tangle of tipsy words and doubts.
'Twas on that gloomy evening, the honest young cashier,
Bespoke him to the manager, and "Sir," said he, "Look
    here,
The staff is nearly idle, and so I think you might
Excuse me now, I'm wanting to do a thing to-night?"

"Well, you may go and do it."   He went, and down he stole
Into the lonely coal-hole, behind a lump of coal,

And trussed him
     like a hedgehog
upon the slack till sure,
He heard the distant
     slamming,
that closed
     the outer door.
Then stole him
     from the coal-hole,
he stole him
     up the stairs,

He ambushed on the landing, for fear of unawares.
He stole into the strong-room, and stealing out his key,
He stole it to the keyhole, and opened cautiously.
He looted off that evening as much as he could hold,
'Twas close on half a million, and all in solid gold.

           *:   *:   *:

'Twas on that self-same evening the chairman thought 'twas
     right,
To work his own manœuvre, 'twas such a roughish night.
Three overcoats were on him, with pockets every side,
Ten carpet bags he carried, and all were deep and wide.
He also had a hatbox, and novel thought, and bright ;
He stitched a row of stockings behind him out of sight.
He loaned a sealskin wallet, a whalebone gingham tent,
And through the garden gate he skid, and down the town he
     went.
He skirmished through the darkness, he skulked against the
     wind,
He spankled by some people, and left them all behind.

He slewed around
a corner,
and up the lane he slank,
And shuffled thro'
the wicket
of the courtyard
of the Bank.
He ducked into
the back door,
and picking up the stair,

He sneaked into the strong room, and, heavens! what was
there?
The iron door was open, and all the heap of gold
Was gone! He sank with horror, and to the floor he rolled.

And from beneath
the tables
and corners of the room,
Three coppers
scrambled on him,
like shadows of his doom.

They put him on his trial,
and heedless of his rank,
He got an awful sentence,
for robbing of the Bank.

It proves that men are mortal, the sequel I have here,
The bankers called a meeting, they called the young cashier.
Said they, " You have impressed us with great integritee,
We'll give the future management of all the Bank to thee."

They made a testimonial, and signed it every one,
'Twas cornered with the pictures of specious deeds he'd done;
And on the scroll in beauty, of art did there appear,
The tribute of their homage to the honest young cashier.

When you prepare for robbing, don't leave your keys about,
For fear a wax impression be taken while you're out ;
And do not come in second, or it might be your doom
To chance upon three bobbies from the corners of the room.

THE ROAD

TO LONDON.

PRETTY maiden, all the way,
          All the way, all the way,
Pretty maiden, why so gay,
          On the road, to London?

" Will you give that rose to me ? "
" That's the flower, of love," said she,
" I'll not give this rose to thee,
          On the road, to London."

" I have got a love, and he,
Is a good heart, true to me,
'Tis for him, this rose you see,
          On the road, to London."

" Where is now, that love ? " asked he,
" He's away from me," cried she,
" But he'll soon return to me,
          On the road, to London."

" Would you know him, an' he be
Waiting there, by yonder tree ? "
" Aye would I, on land or sea,
      Or the road, to London ! "

" Then my sweetest, I am he,
Give that rose of love to me,
I have come, to greet with thee,
      On the road, to London ! "

Then he flung his cloak aside,
" I have come to make a bride,
Of the fairest, far and wide,
      On the road, to London."

Then she laughed at him, and chaffed,
Unromantic, chaffed, and laughed ;
Till he thought, that she was daft,
      On the road, to London.

" No ! " said she " That's not the way,
Parted lovers, meet to-day,
'Tis by note, or wire, they say
   ' On the road, to London.'

" So 'twere best, thou didst by flight,
Take thy footsteps, out of sight,
Lest my love, per fortune, might
   Strike the road, to London !

" We've been having shrimps and tea,
He's a champion knock out ; He
Could knock spots off you," said she,
   On the road, to London.

" See ! my spouse, from yonder gap,
Cometh like a thunder clap ! "

" Ho ! then here's for the first lap !
   On the road, to London."

ANTEDILUVIAN PAT O'TOOLE

And all His Fleet of Sail

THE SHAMROCK

WHILE poking my umbrella into the cracks and crannies that serve to vary the monotonous setting of the stones of a certain Pyramid of Egypt, I scraped away a portion of mortar or cement, and was agreeably surprised, by discovering a roll, of what I fondly hoped might be a bundle of faded Bank of England notes; but on closer inspection, it proved to be a scroll of papyrus, thickly covered with curious hieroglyphics.

They throw a misty light on the history of the O'Tooles, for written in a strange mingling of blank verse, and ballad metre, they purport to give a correct version of the account of the Deluge; in which disaster, it appears that a worthy ancestor of the said family played a conspicuous, and important part.

An Addenda accounting for their presence in the pyramid is appended, and contains the plausible statement, that it was actually a descendant of the said O'Toole, who designed and built the tombs of the Pharoahs, and adopted this subtle means of sending his name down to these remote ages.

Some savants and Egyptologists will cavil at this startling information, but I happen to be in possession of a three cornered cypher that runs thro' the composition of their architecture, which will be of convincing merit, when I have time to issue the seven folio volumes, which I am not preparing at present, in connection with this important subject.

The opening line proves that the Ballad must have been composed at a much earlier period than that of the deluge.

'TWAS in the raal ould antient times, when there wasn't
 any probability
Of thruth at all in anything, before the world was dhrownded,
An' the people spoke in Irish, with a wonderful facility,
Before their undherstandin's wor be foreign tongues
 confounded,
It was just about this pariod of the fine ould anshint history
Of the murnful earth, that Pat O'Toole, the Irishman was born,
    He gev the information,
    In a noisy intimation
Of his presence, rather early, on a Whitsun Monday morn,

But it's not all out particular, or anything material,
To the thruth consarnin' all about the narrative I've spun,
    The story of his birth,
     or the mirth
    Upon this earth,
That shook his father's rafthers, with rousin' rounds of fun.

   *   *   *   *   *

Whin Pat at last had come of age, It took a hundred years
 or so,
  For then the men lived longer, and a minor wasn't free,
    To slip out of the chancery,
    An' from his legal infancy,
    To come into his property,
    Till the end of a century;

Well it was just about that time a floatin' big menagerie,
 Was bein' built by Noah, in the exhibition thrade,—
He advertised, an' posted it, got editorial puffs on it,
 Explainin' that 'twould be the best, that ever yet was
  made.

He had it pasted up on walls, dhrawn out in yalla, red, an'
 green,

A lion tamer too
 Was dhrew,
In puce, an' royal blue,
A hairy bowld gorilla new,
He got from Mossoo Doo Shalloo,
An elephant with thrunk, hooroo !
The plaziozarus, and emu,
 A wild hoopoo,
 A cockatoo,
An' the boxin' kangaroo,
He had it hoarded round, away
From thim that didn't want to pay,
An' guarded all be polis, in a private public park,
He paid a man that cried " Hooray ! "
In shouts you'd hear a mile away,
 " Come in, an' see the menagerie, that's cotch
  for Noah's Ark,
Come look at the wild menagerie, before the flood of wet
 comes down,
For thin ye won't have time to see, ye'll all be dhrownded thin !
 The glass is goin' down to-day
 An' sure from far Americay,
A blizzard's on the thrack I hear, so lose no time, come in ! "

Twas thin O'Toole, the Irishman, pushed wid his elbows
    thro' the crowd,
        He dhropped his tanner, an' he wint into the show
            that day,
An' as he thrapsed along the decks, an' in the howld, an' up
    an' down,
        He sudden got a pleasin' thought, an' thin he went away,
He kep' the saycret to himself, an' never towld a single sowl,
        He kep' it dark, so there was none to budge, or tell
            the tale,
He wint to Father Mooney, an' he took the pledge agin' the
    drink,
        An' in the sheds of his back yard, he built a fleet of sail,
He whistled as he worked, an' took a soothin' whiff of
    honest weed,—
        That wasn't 'dultherated wid cabbage laves, or such,—
            " I'll prove that Noah's out of it,"
            He sung, an' took an airy fit
Of step dancin', " I'll make a hit, an' lave him on a crutch!"
He saw that Noah advertised, in notices around about,
        He'd have to charge the passengers, to save them
            from the flood,
'Twas such a dirty selfish thrick, that nobody could stand to it;
        But like a thrue born Irishman, siz Pat, siz he, " I could
                Collect thim all,
                Both great an' small,
            An' won't give him a chance at all,
I'll spoil his speculation, an' I'll save thim from the flood!"

Wid that he wandhered round the world, an' gathered curiosities,
        Of every sortins of the male, an' of the faymale kind,

An' thin embarked thim in his fleet, until he had them all
     complate,
          He didn't lave a quadruped, or bird, or midge behind,
He kep' the saycret to himself, an' never wint upon the dhrink,
          An' out of every pub, they missed his presence round
               the town,
                    Until the sky was gettin dark,
                    An' thin the hatches of the ark,
          Wor overhauled by Noah, an' the wet kem peltin' down,
Thin Japhet, Shem, an' Ham, stood on the threshowld of
     their father's ark,
          An' shouted to the thousands, that wor in the **teemin'**
               rain,
" Shut up yer umberellas quick, an' save yerselves for half-a-
     crown,
          Ye'll never have a chance like this, in all yer lives again !

                    For if ye want to save yer wives,
                    Or if ye'd like to lave yer wives,
                    Or maybe wish to save yer lives !
                         It's half a crown, come in,
                    The world will all be dhrownded soon !
                    We know it be the risin' moon,
                    A wheel of mist is round her boys,
                    Come in, an' save yer skin ! "
                    The charge was rather high, an' so
                         they didn't get a sowl to go,
                    For thin the royal mint was low,
                    an' everyone was poor,
" Ah ! what's the use of bawlin' there ? " siz Noah, from his
     aisy chair,
          " Yer only blatherin to the air ! come in an' hasp the door,"

Just thin the wathers risin' high, the people all began to cry,
    An' scrambled to the places dhry, as fast as they could
      whail;
Whin all at once they seen a show, for from the distance down
    below,
Came Captain Pat O'Toole hooroo! an' all his fleet of sail!

He scattered life belts in the flood, an' empty casks, an'
    chunks of wood,
      An' everything he possibly could, with nets, an' ropes,
        an' thongs
He dhragged thim in by hook, or crook, a tinker, king, a
    thramp or duke,
      By fishin' line, or anchor fluke, an' several pairs of tongs,
                        L 2

The elephant loaned out
his thrunk,
To male or faymale, in their funk
Of wather,—without whiskey,—
dhrunk ;
An' risin' thro' the wreck
Of the cowld deluge, teemin' round,
Giraffe, an' ostrich, scoured the ground,
An' every dhrownin' sowl they found,
They saved them by a neck !
For Pat was known, to bird, an' baste,
Of kindly heart, an' so a taste,
Of pleasin' gratitude they placed,
For help of Captain Pat,
While fore, an aft, an' every tack,
The captain scrambled like a black,—
With freight of men, his punts to pack—
In specks, an' bright top hat.
On larboard, or on starboard side, whatever dhrownin'
Crowds he spied, he dhragged them in wid wholesale pride,
As quick as jumpin' cat !
The blind an' lame, the short, an' tall, the wild, an' tame,
The great, an' small, wid tubs he came, an' saved them all,
The skinny, round, an' fat.

He didn't care,
At front or rare,
    Or head or tail,
No matther where,
He didn't fail,
By skin, or hair,
Whin once he cotch a grip,

He hawled thim in with frightened howls, upon the decks, as
    thick as rowls;
    Till all the world of livin' sowls, wor safe in every ship!!

He saved the King
    of Snookaroc,
    he had no
    trowsers on,
        its thrue,
But what is that
    to me or you?
    he saved him all the same,
There was no bigotry in Pat,
    an' in the bussel of the king,
He stuck a boat hook, with a spring,
    an' saved him all the same!
The Rooshan Bear he did not shirk,
    he cotch him on a three-
        pronged fork,
And wrastlin' with a furious Turk, he dumped thim on
    the deck,

The Chinese Emperor ;
   he squat
  around a lamp, siz he
    to Pat,
" O Captain take me
   out of that,"
Pat scruffed him be
   the neck,
" O do not save the Jap
   he said,
He has no pigtail on
   his head,

The bad pernicious chap ! "—But Pat hauled in the Jap.

Outside a public house, the sign was loaded with the muses nine,
    They shouted " Pat ah ! throw a line, we've all been on
      the dhrink,"
Siz Pat " Although I'll never brake the pledge meself, here,
  thry an' take
    Howld of the teeth of this owld rake," and raked thim
      in like wink !
Three judges of a county coort, wor by the wathers taken short,
    O throth, it must have been the sport, to see their
      dhreepin' wigs !
" Ketch on to this ! " said Pat O'Toole, an' like a soft, good
  natured fool,
    He flung a lawyer's 'lastic rule, an' dhragged thim in
      like pigs.
We'd all be innocent, in bliss, with ne'er a polis, but for this,
    The judges shouted, " do not miss "—and dashed their
      dhreepin' wigs,

"O save the polismen!" they cried, "There's thirteen on a
    roof outside;"
        An' with some knotted sthrips of hide, he mopped them
            in like pigs,

        "Now ships ahoy!"
           siz Pat, "We may
        Put out to say,
        Without delay,
        An' while its day,
        We'll start away,
      Before the rising gale,"

Thin from a
      bog oak,
  three-legg'd
      stool,
He took the sun,
    with a
  two foot rule,

An' round the world,
           went Pat O'Toole,
An' all his fleet of sail!

'Twas on St. Swithin's day, the wet began, an' rained for
  forty days,
      An' forty nights, it blundhered out the thunder, lift
        an' right,
Whin like a merricle it stopped, the sun came out, said Pat
  O'Toole,
      " Hooroo ! there's land ahoy ! the tops of Wicklow are
        in sight ! "

An' then he brought his ships around, an' dhropped a cargo
  everywhere,
      In counthries where they'd propagate, an' where he
        thought they'd fit,
He made a present to the blacks, of lions and the tigers, and
      The serpents and the monkeys, and such awkward
        perquisit,
He gev the Esquimaux, the bears, an' with the Rooshins,
  left a few,
      An' dhropped a hungry wolf or two, to make the
        bargain square,
The mustang, and the buffaloe, the red man of the wilderness,
      To bowld Amerikay he gev, an' still you'll find thim there,

To Hindoostan, the elephant,
    an' hippopotamus he gev,
The alligator, crocodile,
The simple vulture too,

The divil for Tasmania, the 'possum, an' the parakeet,
    He brought out to Osthreelia, with the boundin' kangaroo.
He left the Isle of Man the last, an' gev a three-legged cat that
    passed
    One day, beneath a fallin' mast, an' cut her tail in two!

The only thing he missed, in this regard of all the captain done,
    He didn't save the Irish elk, 'twas dhrownded be the
        flood,
But still we can't find fault with him, he made it up to
    Erin, for
    He didn't lave a reptile there, an' did a power of good.

But while the Captain, Pat O'Toole, was coastin' round, an'
    dhroppin' men,
    An' elephants, an' butterflies, behind him in his thrack,
The ark with Noah, and his wife, an' childer, sthruck on
    Ararat,
    An' sprung a leak, an' all at once, became a total wrack !

Whin Noah got his specks, an' saw by manes of different
 telegrams,
> How Pat O'Toole had been at work, his heart within
> him sunk,
Siz he unto his Familee, " Let one of you's, sit up for me,"
> Thin slipped around the corner, and he dhrank till he
> got dhrunk.

But Pat O'Toole, he always kep' the pledge, he took before
 the flood,
> He lived for eighteen hundred years, a blameless sort
> of life,
And whin he died, the Hill of Howth was built up for his
 monument,
> And Ireland's eye was modelled out, in memory of his
> wife.

SONNET ON

SHARES.

TO fill his glass as host,
   Was honour I did boast,
      And he spake to me one day, with a smile,

" You wish to make a mark,
Then to my counsel hark,
      In the Co., for which I'm chairman, put your pile."
He was noble, he was good,
Of the upper ten, his blood
      Æsthetic tint of azure, all the while,
      A tone to conjure with,—I put my pile.

The shares went down, O my !
Was not a fool to buy ;
      If I had been a savage on the Nile,
I needn't pen this sonnet, with a sigh !

The Lucky Sixpence

YOU can't exist on nothing, when launched in wedded life—
So a lucky battered sixpence, was all I gave my wife,
And said to her one morning, " When another vessel starts
I'll scoot, and make my fortune, in romantic foreign parts."

And so I went and scooted, but how the thing was done,
Was not like any pic-nic, or passage made for fun.
We had hardly left the Channel, and were in the offing yet,
When the steward heard me snoring in the quiet lazarette.

It wasn't quite successful—the voyage—after this,
And when we got out foreign, I didn't land in bliss.
I worked my passage over, but the captain wasn't kind,
And all I got for wages, was a compliment behind !

And thus I was a failure, my later life was worse,
When twenty years were over, at last I found a purse.
It made me sad, and homesick, and tired of foreign life,
" I'll start," says I, " for Europe, and try and find my wife."

I sought her when I landed, but everything was changed,
And high and low I wandered, and far and near I ranged ;
I put her full description in several ads.—at last
My flag of hope that fluttered, came half-way down the mast.

I went, and I enlisted all in the bluecoat ranks ;
And took to promenading along the Liffey banks.
I made a measured survey of curbstones in the squares,
And prowled behind the corners, for pouncing unawares.

Twelve months of
measured pacing,
had gone since I began;
I hadn't run a prisoner,
the time was all I ran ;
And when the year
had vanished,
said the sergeant,
" Halt, O'Brine !
You haven't run a prisoner, you'll have to draw the line ."

That night I went and drew it—'twas peeping through a
blind !—
I got some information, of suspicious work behind.
The act I had my eye on, was a woman with some lead,
I watched her squeeze a sixpence, in wad of toughened bread.

A chance of some distinction was here, I could not shirk,
I peeled my worsted mittens, and bravely went to work.
I double somersaulted the window —'twas a do
I picked up in Australia, from a foreign kangaroo.

I lighted on the table,
    not quite upon my
    feet,
But, ah! her guilty
    terror was evidence
    complete.
"Wot's this," said I,
    impounding the
    lead, and bread,
    and tin;
" I've caught you in the act, ma'am, I'll have to run you in."

They put her on her trial, and the evidence began,
I swore my information, like a polis and a man;
I showed a silver sixpence, with a hole in it defined,
And showed them how I telescoped my presence thro' the blind.

The jury found her guilty, the judge condemned her then,
To go into retirement, where she couldn't coin again.

"O, sure I wasn't coinin', mavourneen judge asthore,
'Twas the sixpence of my sweetheart that's on a foreign shore.

A lucky one he gave me, he stayed away too long.
I wanted for to change it, and thought it wasn't wrong
To take its little photograph, for the sake of bein' his wife."
Said the Judge, " It doesn't matter, I've sentenced you for
     life ! "

I saw her disappearing, from my eye behind the dock,
O, ham an fowl! it's awful, to think upon the shock.
I staggered with my baton to the sergeant, and I swore,
He had made me run too many, I'd seek a foreign shore.

A Wall Flower Sonnet

SHE was charming, full of grace,
        A hostess, you could place
In a higher sphere, than that in which she shone,
" I've a partner you should meet,
A girl, extremely sweet ! "
And for the dance she always put me on,
But meetings of regret,
Were maidens that I met,
My hostess was a gay designing
        one,
Her wallflowers were too plain,
The waltz did give me pain,
I took a B. and S. and I was
        gone !
She played with me, too often
        put me on,
My hostess was a gay designing
        one !

HE was up on the hustings, and thrashed with his
          tongue,
      The air in a socialistic vein,
And as an employer, for the workers he felt,
      By proxy,—a sympathetic pain!
A pang, that the few could wallow in their wealth,
      Whilst many—their brothers—should sweat,
" But ha!" shouted he, with a chuckle, and a grin,
      " You'll be having a millenium of it yet!"

He taught that the masters should share with the men,
      He scouted, with pitiless vim,
The right of the master, to more than his man,
      For his man was the master of him,
Then they flourished their hats, for the precept, with hope,
      That to practice, he might be content;
But the confidence trick, is a hustings resource,
      And to part, wasn't just what he meant:
He spoke, as a speech is the fashion to-day,

                                                M

In loud paradoxical words,
As a titled Premier of the Commons, would shout,,
      " Down down with the House of Lords."
But still, 'twas a hopeful, and beautiful proof,
      That the cause of the toiler, was just,
And he wouldn't have to wait, very long for a snack,
      From the sugar ornamented upper crust,
In a very little time, he'd be gathering his whack,
      From the azure-fired diamond—upper dust,
" You'll be having a millenium of it yet, working men,
      Put me into Parliament, and then,
You'll find it a fact, we'll pass every act,
      For your chums, and your kids, working men,
The hours you will work, will be eight, working men,
      On Saturday, not quarter so late,
And another holiday, in the middle of the week,
      We'll give you, by the laws of the state,
      With a capon, or a duck, on your plate,
      O put me into Parliament, and *wait !*
You'll be having the land parcelled out into bits,
      You'll be all of you fixed in the soil,
And spontaniety of crops you will reap,
      Without any trouble or toil.
The screw will extend for each working man,
      Employers will have to screw back,
Till tailored by the act, in polished top hats,
      You'll all be as gents in the track !
We'll cut away the taxes, by the laws that we'll pass !
      You won't have to pay any rate !
You'll be having a millenium of it yet, working men,
      O put me into Parliament, and *wait !* "

And thus with emotional foliated flights,
          He spoke like the clashing of swords,
As a titled Premier of the Commons would shout,
      . " Down down with the House of Lords ! "

He finished his speech in a thunder of cheers,
          The welkin was knocked into splits,
And he smuggled off home, by the rear, or his trap,
        They'd have looted for souvenir bits !

   ☆   ☆   ☆   ☆   ☆   ☆   ☆

With the conscience of one, who believes he has done,
        What was really the best, for himself,
He retired into bed, that night, and he fell
        Fast asleep, like a saint on a shelf.

It might have been a very short period of time,
        Or maybe it might have been long,
When he woke with a buzz like a bee in his ear,
        Or the purr of a tom cat's song.
It might be the bizz of a wasp, or the hum,
        Of a foraging blue bottle fly,
But no ! 'twas the sound of the whizz of a drill !
        'Twas then that he opened his eye.

He jumped up in bed, and he cried with an oath,
        " What's that, that you're doing, you scamp ? "
To a burglar brave, who was sampling his room,
        With a bag, jemmy, brace, and a lamp.
Then the burglar grinned in an amicable way,
        For a diplomatic cracker was he,
And he wouldn't take offence at the oath of a man,
        Who had only awoke, said he,

" I was down at the meetin' an' heerd every word,
       When you gave out the socialist pay,
An' I am a bloke wot swears by the truth
       Of the beautiful words that you say.
That's whoy I am here, for my slice of the swag,
       That you've pinched, by employin' your men.
I'm tottin' up the stock, in a confidential way,
       For an equal division of it then,
For mate, I'm a pal of a Socialistic turn,
       Wot tries to do everythink straight,
We'll halve them between us, the jewels and coin,
       An' make an even deal of the plate."

But out from the bed,
       with a jump in his shirt,
The candidate
       sprang to the floor,
Said he, " I may preach,
       but to practice is bosh ! "
       And leaped
with a shout to the door.
But the cracker of cribs,
       with a colt in his fist,

Was first, and with that at the nose
Of the candidate, muttered " You'll die of the cold,
       If you don't burrow under the clothes !

"So don't make a row," said that burglar brave,
       " But jerk into bed out of sight,
I hate to be put upon when I'm at work,
       An' Boss, this is my busy night !

"Now jest let me fasten a gag on yer mouth,
      You know that it's wrong, to alarm
Your neighbours at night, when they're wantin' to sleep,
      Quick! into this noose with each arm,
There! now, with that beautiful knot on your pins,
      You cawn't say as how yer to blame,
If I pinch all I can in the regular way,
      Of the grabber's contemptible game!"

He opened the safe, and he smashed the bureau,
      He looted the drawers, and shelf,
Of the plate, and the clocks, and the watches, and cash,
      From the cabinet, quick as an elf.
Slid everything down to his pal, with a rope,
      And then he slid down it himself,
They drove with the swag, from the terrace amain,
      In a couple of hired out traps;
And the city, was billed on the following day,
      With the Special Editions in caps!

   *   *   *   *   *   *   *

'Twas a reasonable period, from the incident above,
      That a solemn deputation came down,
For the candidate to speak in a socialistic vein,
      To the voters of the east of London town:
"We'll be looking for you there, on waggon No. I.
      Near the arch, that's of marble, in the park,"
But he pointed to the door "O tell them that I'm dead;
      For cram it! I am not up to the mark,"

A CANTABILE ON

MUSIC, ART, AND LAW.

Ho! there, pumps and castanets for three,
We would dance a brief measure.

O YOU will wonder why we're here,
        And wish that we were far,
By wig, and gown, it doth appear,
        We're members of the bar,
And tho' we are, we say to you,
        We all of us opine,
That we may justly claim our due,
        In an artistic line.
We are the type of one, you know,
        As well as we can tell,
He is a burly splendid beau,
        A stately howling swell !—
A signor of the lyric stage,
        An operatic Don,—
And by similitude, we'll wage
        That he, and we are one !

'Tis true, tho' he is mostly stout,
       We're nearly always thin,
But if you turn us inside out,
       We're stouter men within.
For he is all a puff, and smoke,
       A sound that dies away;
But we are they who crack a joke,
       That lasts for many a day.

He has his crotchets; we do harp,
       On clients, this, and that,
He has his sharps, and we are sharp,
       His flats, and they are flat ;
He blows away his notes, but we,
       Are shrewder men by far,
The notes we get professionly,
       We stick them to the Bar !

His quavers, they are nothing to
       The rallantando thrills,
That shake our clients, when we screw
       The rosin on their bills.
They often simulate, as deaf,
       When we do charge a case,
Our time is on the treble cleff,
       And their's is on the base.

We make a loud fortissimo,
       When pleading in the wrong,
And often pianissimo,
       When we should put it strong,

But still we pull our fees the same,
          Tho' suits may not be won,
And by our tongue, we conquer fame,
          Like that conceited Don.

And to the jury, we do plaint,
          Upon a mauling stick,
And from our pallets, clap the paint,
          Around their craniums thick,
We mould them from their purpose dense,
          Like hods of plastic wax,
And sculp into their common sense,
          And then climb down their backs !

Our song is done, for we are brief,
          And we will sing no more,"—
And to my own intense relief,
          I thought they'd take the door,
But no ! they did not go, and each,
          Put forth his kidded fist,
" While we've been trying thus to teach,
          Our fees we almost missed !

Remember this is Christmas eve,
          Three Chrismas waits we be,
The more the reason you should give,
          Our consultation fee.
We have our instruments, and they
          Are of the parchment tough,
With which we play, while men do pay,
          We wot we've said enough.

And wherefore, and whereas for this,
       Aforesaid, told to thee,
Moreover, we must have, we wis,
       Our consultation fee.
Five guineas unto each of us,
       Refreshers each, a pound,"—
I rose to kick them into bruss,
       They bolted through the ground !

My future suppers, must be free
       Of nightmare risk ; the cause
Of that cantabile of glee,
       On music, art, and laws ;
Was merely this, that I did run,
       The danger of such rig,
By feeding on a goose, they hatched,
       Inside a lawyer's wig.

WOMAN'S

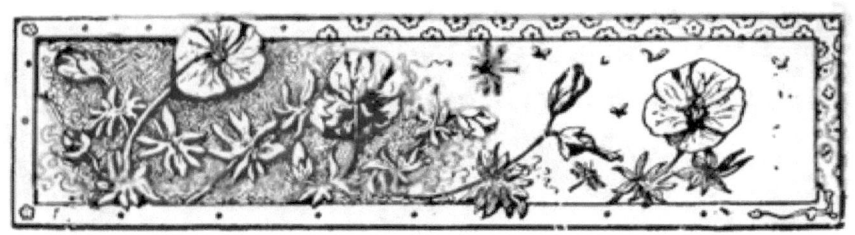

TEARS.

HE tears were in her eye,
   Said I "what makes you cry?"
And my sympathy was such,
            that I sighed;
For it gives my heart the creep,
   To see a woman weep,—
Especially the one to be my Bride.

   "Alas!" said I, "Ah! me,
      It grieveth me, to see
That trickle, at your nostril, by the side.'

" 'Twas the onions, I was cutting," she replied.

HERADIC FRUIT OF A FAMILY TREE

BY A LYIN' KING OF ARMS

W HEN Cha, the first,
          Was run to ground,
An Ancestorial
          Mite was found;
By Rails in Pale,
          At Dexter Chief,
From Judges' wig,
          He pipes his grief.

HIS deeds, of later
       Life, did tend,
To prove him of
       The Sinister Bend;
As boozing Charge,
       He takes his place,
From Sinister Chief,
       To Dexter Base.

H IS son, did Charge
              In Sable Chief,
A Sword, or he
              Had come to grief;
That Chief above,
              From Sinister, part,
Has got,—per Fesse—
              That Sword in Heart !

A NOTHER Son,
        Of prudent parts,
Doth Pawn his Arms,
        For peaceful arts;
From Dexter or,
        On Shield of Gu,
In pale, reguardant
        Sinister Jew.

A NOTHER Son,
          From want appeald,
To art, for Charge,
          On Argent Shield,
And so, upon
          His Coat he drew
A Garb, that he
          Might dare, and do

HE sought to Void
   A hen-coup, he
Is Trussed above it,
   On a tree;
Couchant, in Chief,
   With Spade, in Fesse,
A sorry wight,
   He must confess.

A T length, an Orient
            Pile, he took,
Then Counterchanged,
            His Coat for luck !
This Dexter treatment,
            Is not right ;
He's Or, on Ar,
            The lawless wight !

BUT ah! at last,
          His fate was healed
And by command,
          Got Royal Shield;
A Dexter King,
          Reguardant, won!
He dyed, and left
          An "only Son."

N2

THE POLIS AND THE PRINCESS GRANAUILLE

THE man who confidently seeks to set up a new idea, by upsetting an old theory, or tradition, is one who lives in advance of his time, whereby he forfeits many valued amenities of contemporaneous courtesy. But he is to be extolled for the moral heroism that impells him, to advance new facts, into the study of history, or explode errors so steadfastly grounded on the popular belief, that he finds himself, pen to pen with a hostile army of Savants, Antiquarians, Historians, and Critics; some stirred with spirit of envy, others with a craving for notoriety, but all unanimous, and up in arms, with loaded pens and arsenal of inkpots.

In this regard I find myself, by placing the correct revision of a popular tradition before my discerning readers.

I have to confess that it was not thro' deep and industrious research, that I am thus enabled to challenge the truth, of the accepted records.

It was thro' the chance, afforded by an hour of breezing sea-scape recreation, that I discovered the mysterious chronicle.

The popular tradition, is thus related by Dr. Walsh. "The celebrated Grana Uille or Grace O'Mally, noted for her piratical depredations in the reign of Elizabeth, returning on a certain time from England, where she had paid a visit to the Queen, landed at Howth, and proceeded to the castle. It was the hour of dinner—but the gates were shut. Shocked at an exclusion so repugnant to her notions of Irish hospitality, she immediately proceeded to the shore, where the young lord was at nurse, and seizing the child, she embarked with, and sailed to Connaught, where her own castle stood.

After a time, however, she restored the child ; with the express stipulation, that the gates should be thrown open, when the family went to dinner—a practice which is observed to this day."

WHEN the Hill of Howth was covered, by a city great, and
     grand,
And nuggets still were gathered, like cockles on the strand ;
On the shore, around by Sutton, a children's maid was met,
Who was wheeling of a baby, in a sky blue bassinet.

And as that maiden cycled that infant by the sea,
Down the boreen from the Bailey, came number 90 B ;
And he sudden lit his eye on, he sudden had her set,
That slavey, with the baby, in the sky blue bassinet.

He held aloft his baton, saluted like a man,
Said he " I'm almost certain, you're name is Mary Anne,
The sergeant up the boreen, in the distance there is gone,
We'll make the distance greater, if you and I move on.

For fifty years I've ambushed, and watched around me bate,
But never met a sweetheart, that took me so complate,
And what's a bate ? it's nothin' to a polis, whin he's gone !
I'm gone on you me darlin', let you and I move on."

" O hoky smoke ! avourneen, I never seen yer like,
As sure's me name is Dooley, with the christian name of Mike,
I sware it, by this number, on my collar, which you see,
I'm shockin' fond of you agra," said No. 90 B.

He took that trusting maiden, to the adjacent strand,
" A punt is on the shingles, convaynient here to hand,
Put the bassinet into it," said the blue official fox,
" We'll go and look for winkles, thro' seaweed on the rocks."

Now whether or for winkles, or what it was they went,
They stayed away much longer than was their first intent,
A thoughtless time, that stranded them in a piteous plight,
The tide was in, O Moses! the punt was out of sight.

Upon that woeful morning, the fact we may not shunt,
The little Lord St. Lawrence, was kidnapped by a punt,
And reverbrated wailings, of his nurse is echoed still,
With oathings of the polis, around Ben Heder hill!

But then it struck that polis, a hopeful thought of mark,
And to the weeping servant, he muttered, " Whist! an' hark!"
Then put his index finger, abaft his coral nose,
" Howld on! I'll go, an' square it, I've got a schame, here
      goes!"

The crafty rogue departed, and told the specious tale,
Of how the child was stolen by the Princess Granauille,
He told the weeping mother, he almost thought he knew,
From information he received, that he had got a clew,

When Granauille was challenged, it struck her, she could
      make
A profitable bargain, in re her nephew's sake,
'Twas just before his teething; his nose was but a blob,
Like every other baby's, so she could work the job.

As tourist come from Connaught, she owned that it befel,
That she had left her galley, to find a cheap hotel,
But when she reached the castle, with appetite, it shocked
Her, when she found the outer door, at dinner time was locked!

She thought it mean, and stingy, the child she lifted then—
And told that subtle polis, she'd give the child again,
In safety to its father, if he would leave the door,
At dinner, always open, on the latch for evermore.

Upon Lord Howth, she fathered her nephew in this way,
That he might be ancestor of Viscount Howth to-day,
And if you want a dinner, I'll give you all a tip,
There's just a fleeting moment, I've always let it slip,—

The minute hand records it, upon the castle clock,
And if you're up that moment, you have no need to knock,
Walk in, the door is open, and make "a hearty male,"
And thank that crafty polis, and the Princess Granauille.

   ✢   ✳   ✤   ✢   ✳   ✤   ✳

And now about the baby,
    his voyaging began,
Before he'd had his teething,
    and still he's not a man,

He's yet a child!
    whose ravings
Across the ocean flew,

Of "Who am I? and where am I? and what am I to do?"

He's never grown a whisker, he's never known a beard !
Of hair upon the cranium, he never yet has heard !
And so he is not altered, he's still in statu quo,
As bald and snub, and chubby, as three hundred years ago!

Three hundred years are over, and lo ! he's living yet,
He made a sleeping cabin, from the sky blue bassinet,
He made the punt commodious, with wreckage that he found,
But of a human sinner, he's never heard a sound !

He lives without a purpose, an object or intent,
Three hundred years of waiting, in ignorance are spent,
He lives ; and for this reason, because he never knew,
Of who he is, or where he is, or what he is to do !

He never saw a sailor ! he never hailed a sail !
The pensive penguin harkened unto his lonely wail ;
The albatross did follow he shrieked him for the clew,
" O who am I ? and where am I ? and what am I to do ? "

He pleaded to the swallow, and Mother Cary's chicks,
Of his expatriation, and in his devilish fix,
Besought the mild octopus, and all the ocean crew,
" O who am I ? and where am I ? and what am I to do ? "

He hailed
the great sea serpent,
the   comprehensive
whale,
The flying fish,
        to answer,
the burden of his wail,

Of what the deuce had happened, that life was all so blue !
" O who am I ? and where am I ? and what am I to do ? "

He is not dead, it's certain, I'll merely mention here,
He may be in mid ocean, or yet he may be near,
The north wall boat may hail him, it's prophesied that yet,
He'll be thrown up at Sutton, in the sky blue bassinet.

Be watching all the papers ; for soon or late some day,
In leaded type, you'll see it, and with a big display
Of capitals above it, of claimant, who will know,
Of what to do, and do it, and one who'll have to go !

Now most of you will question, the record I recite,
To clear your doubts upon it, I think it's only right,
To tell you, I was searching for cockles at Blackrock,
When lo ! my heart was fluttered with interesting shock !

I saw a feeding bottle, that lay upon the strand,
I stooped anon and gripped it, with sympathetic hand,
I thought it might be jetsam, of baby that was drowned,
But looking thro' the bottle, a manuscript I found.

And there in broken Irish, it states the fact, that he
Had sealed it in his bottle, and still he's on the sea,
With anxious intimation, that yet he seeks the clew,
Of who he is ? and where he is ? and what he is to do ?

A HORROR OF LONDON TOWN.

O^N London streets by a gin shop door,
    In the blaze of a noontide sun,
With horrible zest of a thirst for gore,
    Was a desperate murder done,
On the sainted flags of a Christian town,
    I saw this outrage planned,
And three little boys, in crime, sere brown
    Were there with a helping hand.

'Twas a group of seven—I counted them all,
    A group of seven strong men,
And summing them up, with the criminals small,
    Their total I think was ten,
With umbrellas, and sticks, and stones,
    They hunted a sad wretch down,
Mid random of kicks, and ogerous groans,
    A shame unto London town!

But while was fought the unequal fight,
    That murder of ten to one,
There came an ominous venger of right,
    They call him a copper for fun,
And I said he'll be pulling the lot of them; then
    The villians ha! ha! shall see
There are dungeons dark for the murderous ten,
    In the walls of the Old Bailee!

But no! He paused, and he gravely stood,
        And the never a stir, stirred he,
As he saw them compass the deed of blood,
        To its end with a ghastly glee,
And O 'twas pity to hear the tones,
        Of the suppliant's voice in pain,
As he sought to fly from the sticks and stones,
        And the yells of " Hit, hit him again!"

A drayman flourished the butt of his whip,
        I am sure it was loaded with lead,
And his laugh was wild, as a terrible clip,
        He aimed at the victim's head!
Alas! too sure, by the jugular vein,
        He was struck, and he dropped and died,
And the drayman shook, as he laughed amain,
        For blood was the caitiff's pride!

But O I proved, ere I wandered home,
        There yet was a friend most true,
Who bore the corse to a silent tomb,
        Ah! yes, and embalmed it too,
A kind purveyor came walking by,
        And he stopped on the edge of the flag,
Then turned to his boy, and exclaimed with a sigh,
        " Jim, slip the dead rat in your bag."

MET him one night there,
North east of Leicester
          Square,
Within about a quarter of a
          mile,

" I've confidence," said he,
" In all humanity,
I'll leave my bloomin' purse
          with thee awhile ! "

He left it, went away
Then coming back, " I say,"
          Said he, with an insinuating smile,
" Now lend your watch to me,
          For I am like yourself without no guile,"
He took it, went away,
And from that evil day,
          I keep that man's description on my file.

A TRAM CAR GHOST.

THE last car at night, is a vehicle laden with varied symptoms of mysterious hauntings that more or less oppress the fares, some toned down by the lassitude of overwork, drop gratefully into their seats, and quickly fall into fitful slumber, others seem to court a spasmodic notoriety by loud and disjointed converse. A weary of world expression clouds the features of a few with an unuttered protest, for the disagreeable fact of their birth, whilst others seem by their grumpy glances to suggest a jealous objection to other people's existence.

A select few, unconsciously advertise a flippant gratification at the possession of life, and squeeze festivity from it, as colour from a blue rag. But all are haunted with the mysterious workings of unseen spirits, that usually accompany the fares, in the latest car at night.

THERE wasn't a soul in the tramway car,
  Well not that myself could see,
But the sad conductor took my arm,
  And steadfast gazed on me—
Then pointing up to the corner seat,
  " Look ! that's his regular game,
I'm sorry to have it to say of a ghost,
  But he hasn't a tint of shame ! "

You'll think the tram conductor was drunk,
  His breath was sweet as mine,
Like the orris root, or a tint of mint,
  Or scent of a similar line.

It might be a ginger cordial; but
        The air of the night was strong,
And it wouldn't be proper to say I'm sure,
        I might perhaps be wrong.

"Will you slack?" said I, but he caught my arm,
        "The man that I killed is there!
I hate to have it to say.   But no,
        I can't recover my fare!
I asked it from him one winter's night,
        But full as a tick with drink,
The only answer he gave to me,
        Was just a chuckle and wink.
With this American tink-a-ting,
        I couldn't defraud the Co.,
So caught his collar, and chucked him off
        The back of the tram car, so.

There wasn't a soul that saw the deed,
        Not even the driver knew,
And there he lay on the tramway track,
        Till the townward car was due.
It broke his neck, and his shoulder blade,
        His legs, and arms, its broke,
And laid him out, a squirming trout,
        'Twas then he awoke, and spoke!

Said he, "What's up? is the dancing done?
        The waltz has made me sore!"
And wriggling out on the frosty ground,
        He never spoke no more!

Heigho ! the murder was caused by me,
        Was never a soul who knew,
That I am the man, who chucked the man,
        That the townward tram car slew !

And everybody on earth was done
        With the murdered man, but me !
The very next night, in the corner seat,
        I looked, and there was he !
I thought at first that he might be a twin,
        And asked his thruppeny fare,
But he sneered at me, I turned away,
        And left him sneering there !
Thinks I, I'll watch him, and jot my tot,
        And when he is goin' to go,
I'll chuck him the same, as I did before,
        For sake of the tramway co.

I calculated the list of fares,
        Then turned around to look,
But hey ! I'm blowed, if he hadn't gone off,
        Gone ! with his bloomin' hook !

But how it was done, or whither he went,
        I never could guess, or think,
For the ventilators all were shut,
        There wasn't an open chink !

And I was up at the door so tight,
        He couldn't have passed me by,
I never did close an eye that night,
        No lid of a bloomin' eye !

I hates to see the company done,
         And that was a cheated fare,
I'd rather lose my regular meals,
         Than wrong the company, there !
I'd rather work from ante M, six
         Till three of the A.M. clock,
Than wrong the tramway co. of a coin,
         That wasn't my legal stock.
There's nobody sees the ghost but me,
         Because he's a sneaking sprite,
He always comes when I take my turn
         On the latest car at night.
That's him ! he's there in the corner seat,
         The man that I killed is there,
I hate to have it to say, But no,
         I can't recover my fare !
I've this American tink-a-ting,
         And tickets of sortin's three,
But that embezzling raw will come
         To cheat, and sneer at me.

I cawnt tell why, but he worry's me so,
         I'd collar him if I could,
He hasn't a scruff, or any a crop,
         O' the neck, or flesh or blood,

He hasn't a waistband, I could grip,
         Nor anythink I could kick,
I'd like to fetch him a trip, but ah !
         To think of it, makes me sick

He hasn't a face, to black his eye,
        Or even a hat to block,
But all the same, in the corner there,
        He gives the fares a shock !
He dosses himself in the favourite seat,
        And while he's nestlin' there,
The passengers cawnt shove up to the end,
        To make my regular fare.

For some insist that the seat is cold !
        And others complain it's hot !
And some it's damp, and some remark,
        It's a most infernal spot !
And some keep shovin' their sticks above,
        To let in the atmosphere,
While others are closin' them up with a curse,
        The thing is devilish queer.

It's pisonous hard on a man like me,
        Who lives on what he can get,
But I'll have to try and see if I cawnt,
        Jest manage to shuffle him yet.

Ha ! there, he's gone ! I knew that he would,
        Waltz out of my bloomin' sight !
His regular trick with my thruppeny fare,
        Now —jump with the car, good night."

o

MARGATE
SANDS.

HE was five, or six, he four years old,
  When they met on the Margate Sands,
And he gravely looked in her great blue eyes
  With hold of her little fat hands,
And he said, " I love oo well Rosie ;
  I know, dat I'd rather have oo,
Dan all de lickel girls on de sands to-day,
  Iss, even dan de girl in blue ! "

" I'm glad oo do ; and I love oo too ! "
  Thro' a heaven of golden hair,
Like silvery bells, was her sweet response,
  On the ozoned rose lit air,
And then with his bucket, and spade, he built
  For his love, on the sand, that day,
A castle, and pie, till the tide came in,
  And washed his castle away.

 :   :   :   :   :   :   :

In many a year thereafter 'twas,
  In a box in Drury Lane,
Said a gent, as he used his opera glass,
  " Yon lady's remarkably plain ! "
And the lady exclaimed, at the self-same time,
  When she saw his glass in hand,
" What an ugly fright ! " they did not know,
  They had loved, on the Margate sand !

JOHN McKUNE

O PADDY MURPHY—
    carman of the stand
    in College Green—
You've had your sudden
    ups and downs, and busy
    days you've seen,
    We're waiting for your story;
how the mare struck up the tune,
    Of sparks amongst the gravel,
on the road to Knockmaroon.

    " O faith an' I may tell you,
    you will not be waitin' long,
Whin the piebald mare Asooker, is the sweetheart of me song,

02

For sure it was a mastherpiece, of how she dhragged McKune,
Behind her whiskin' tail, along the road, to Knockmaroon.

'Twas in the busy period, whin the Fenians wor at war,
I mopes'd around the Dargle, on a newly painted car;
Whin, creepin' from the ditches, like a bogey in the moon,
A man proposed the journey of a dhrive to Knockmaroon.

He might as well have axed me on the minute, for a run,
To Roosha or to Paykin, or the divil or the sun!
He might as well have axed me, for a Rocky Mountain jaunt;
So I bounced him with an answer of the sudden words, "I
    can't!"
The boys to-night are risin' an' I darn't go impugn
Me car into the danger, of a dhrive to Knockmaroon!"

Thin spakin' wid the dacency, of a remorseful tone,
" In fact," siz I, " me car's engaged, in Bray, by Mick Malone;
Besides the mare is nervous, an' me wife expects me soon,
For the army's out, I hear, upon the road to Knockmaroon!"

He didn't stop to parley, but he jumped upon me car,
An' showed a livin' pixture, of the brakin' of the war,
By pointin' a revolver at me nose!   "I'm John McKune,
Dhrive   on,"   siz   he,   "I'll   guard   you   on   the   road   to
      Knockmaroon!"
I never knew that powdher smelt so flamin' strong before,
It smelt as if a whole review, was stinkin' from the bore!
The steel of that revolver shone, like bayonets in the moon,
Of all the British army on the road to Knockmaroon!
An' hauntin' round its barrel, the ghosts of every sin,
I done in all me life before, wor there, in thick an' thin!
So like a fiddler in a fight I quickly changed me tune,
" Bedad!" siz I, "It's I'm yer man, we're off to Knockmaroon."
" You see, I've got a takin' way," says he, an' with a grin,
He put his barker back into his breeches fob, agin,
" Now whail around, an' thro' the bog,—the feather bed,"—
      says he,
" I'll guard you, by the barracks of the Polis, at Glencree,
An' dhrive, as if yer car was late, to bring the Royal Mail!
Whip up! as if the divil sat upon your horse's tail!"

I gev the mare a coaxer, of the knots upon me whip,
An' rowlin thro' the darkness, where the road begins to dip,
I bowled upon me journey, with the load of John McKune,
An' fits of wondher, why he dhrove that night to Knockmaroon;
An' just as we were wheelin' out, beyond the feather bed,
The boys put up their lamplight, an' alightin' down, he said
Some hurried words an' whisperin's, then with a cheer for
      him,
Presentin' arms, " Dhrive on," they cried, "God speed you
      Wicklow Jim!"

I dhrove as if the Phooka was the horse beneath me whip,
We flew, as if the jauntin' car was on a racin' thrip,
We scatthered dust, an' whizz of wheels, an' sparks upon the
    air,
When all at once, I pulled her up, at shout of "Who comes
    there ? "
It was a throop of sojers, an' me heart began to croon,
Wid jigs, aginst me overcoat ! siz he, " I'm John McKune,"—
He sprang from off the cushion, an' a little while was gone,
Then comin' back, a captain gev the password, to dhrive on !

He leaped upon the car again, an' says to me, once more,
" Now, dhrive me 'cross the grand canal, and on to Inchicore,"
But when we got around a turn, an' in a lonely place,
He whipped his waypon out again, to point it at me face !
Siz he, " Yer car is weighty, an' yerself's a dacent bulk,
You say the mare is nervous, an' she might begin to sulk ;
We mustn't let that meddle with the work that I've in hand,
So skip your perch this minute, like a lark, at my command,
Come, hop yer twig, unyoke her, in a slippy lightenin' crack !
Just double up that rug, an' sthrap it tight across her back,
An' shorten up the reins, an' swop yer overcoat an' hat,
Quick ! flutther up, as if you wor a blackbird from a cat ! "

I never felt so brave, in all me life, me courage rose,
To bid him go to blakers !—but the barrel at me nose,
Brought down me heart like wallop, till I felt it, in me brogue,
An' so I done his dirty work, the ugly thievin' rogue !
I loosed the crather from the shafts, and sthrapped the rug,
    an' then,
He vaulted on her back, an' faced her up the road again,

" You'll find her in the mornin', on the grass in Phœnix Park,"
He shouted, as with skelpin' whip, he galloped thro' the dark,
An' left me cursin' in a fit, beside me sthranded yoke,
As if I got the headache of a mapoplectic sthroke !

Next night, whin I was frettin', that I'd never see her more,
I heard the mare Asooker's hoof, beside the stable door ;
I darted out, she kissed me, with a whinney loud and long,
That made her ever afther, as the sweetheart of me song !

  *   *   *   *   *   *   *

When fifteen years wor over, an' meself was down in Cork,
I read it on a paper,—in the Bowry of New York,—
Of a pub around a corner, where a lonely man in June,
Was sittin', when two men came in, says they, " you're John
  McKune ! "

He dhropped his glass of cock-tail, with a crash upon the floor;
And looked, as if he'd jump the sash, of window, or the door,
He looked, as if he'd rather be in Hell, or on the moon ;
Said they, " At last we have you, for a traitor, John McKune ! "

He didn't spake an answer, but he quickly thried to grip,
The bright revolver waypon, from the fob, behind his hip,
He hadn't time to dhraw it, like a flashin' lightenin' dart,
Two loaded levelled weapons, wor against his jumpin' heart!

"Hands up!" they shouted "Damn you! ye scaymin' divil's
    limb;
We've come to scotch the serpent, we know as Wicklow
    Jim,"
Said they, "At last we have you for oaths you gave to men,
An' swore them for your purpose, to bethray, an' sell them
    then!"

He didn't make an answer, but he thried to whip a knife,
From collar of his cota—it was there to guard his life—
He hadn't time to dhraw it, for a crack of shots! an' soon,
A pool of blood, was spurtin' from the corpse of John McKune.

I'LL GO FOR A SOJER.

" O WHERE is my Johnnie acushla?" says she,
  He left me last night, an' " Maggie " says he,
" It's meself an' yerself mam that couldn't agree,
        Be dang but I'll go for a sojer!"

He took all the cash that I had in the till,
I followed him round to the butt of the hill,
" Go back, or yerself is the first that I'll kill!"
        Says he, " Whin I'm gone for a sojer!"

I hung to his neck, an' I axed him to stay,
Ye might as well ax for the night to be day;
But wringin' his neck from me, shoutin' " Hooray!"
        Says he " Whoo! I'll go for a sojer!'

I set the dog afther him, thought that he'd stick
In the tail of his coat, he was up to the thrick;
For he turned on his heel, an' he skelped him a lick,
        Of the stick, " I am off for a sojer!"

"O whisht ! arrah there, look he's comin' ! " she cried,
As far in the distance, her Jack she espied,
With Corporal Quirk on the march by his side,
　　　　　He's comin' back home with a sojer.

When Johnnie came near enough to her to spake,
"O Johnnie Avourneen ! " said she, " did ye take
The shillin' ? "　" No faith, for I'm too wide awake,
　　　　　I only wint off for a sojer."

ODE HERE!

I DYED away the grey, from my sparsy head of hair,
　　　　　I buttered up the fur upon my tile,
I darned the ventilators in my garments here, and there,
　　　　　And with my go-to-meeting stick, and smile,
I went to see a widow, I had courted long ago ;
　　　　　She had just been to the Probate for a pile!

Said she, " You are a person that I really do not know "
　　　　　Her tone was rather cutting, like a file !
　　　　　A serious alteration in her style ;
　　　　　I knew her when a maiden without guile,
　　　　　She wouldn't even loan me from her pile,
　　　　　A widow's mite ; it agitates my bile !

THE SMUGGLER'S FATE

A Seaside Idyll this ;
To teach how oft amiss,
Doth fall the fate of men
who would be free :

It makes me cry heigho,
In minor cadence low,
When I do mind me
Of the fate of three,

To shun hymenial perils,
And tired of mashing girls,
A smuggler's cave, they took beside the sea,

And formed a reckless crew,

That swallowed their own brew,

    Of whiskey, punch and coffee, beer and tea;

    But most of beer, and whiskey, as you see,

And that's the reason that I cry heigho!

They wrestled with the wave,

Then ran into their cave;

But telescopes above, were taking stock,

Thus fate was on their track,

And soon alas! alack!

The smiles of fate fell on them from the rock,

Thus mesmerised by mirth,

They climbed the rocks, and earth,

   With fascinated recklessness alack !

My sympathy to show,

Again I say heigho !

   'Twere better to their cave they had gone back.

Ah ! me, the smugglers three,
Were blind their fate to see,
    And lo ! capitulation followed soon ;

For spite of all their pains,
They soon were in the chains,
    That fettered them in bondage 'neath the moon,

That shone on double case, of treble spoon ;
Too like the moon, that wanes ;
    And that is why I sing in minor tune,
And cry again with sympathy, heigho !

P

Thus ever day by day,
In bondage still they lay,
    Surrendering provisions, and their brew,

Until the crew did go
Into the town, and lo !

A parson had some triple work to do,

They're captives now,

hard labour is their due,

Alack ! the hapless crew ;

I cry again with sympathy, heigho !

THE LATE
FITZ-BINKS.

I T was about an hour they call the small, and the mysterious,
  An hour wherein the ghosts are wont to take their
   constitutional,
'Twas twenty-four o'clock ; an hour that's oftimes deleterious
  To many a liver wetted swell, pugnacious or emotional.
The beggared corporation lights, did flick in the nor'wester
  gale,
   That blistering nose, and finger-tips, were loaded well
    with sleet,
When Binks harrangued a constable, " Good night, it's cold,
  you're looking pale,"
   From where he backed a lamp-post, at the end of
    Brunswick Street.
" Ah! Sergeant," said Fitz-Binks, "It's late, or I could
  treat you decently,
   And 'twouldn't be too dusty, if we had a flying drink ;
But Chap, of Vic., is strict, they passed in Parliament so
  recently,"
   The bobbie was a thirsty one, he winked a thirsty wink.
" Ha! ha!" said Binks, " You know the lines, so don't be
  too particular,
   There's some back door that's open," said the
    constable, " you're right ;
Just move an' there thro' yondher lane an' hide up perpendicular,
   Beyant the lamp, I'll folly whin there's nobody in sight."

The thing was managed gracefully, and with an open sesamè,
    The constable had stolen to a quiet bar with Binks,
Produced a clay, said he, " I hope yer honor won't think
    less of me,
        To pull a pipe," " By Jove ! I don't," said Binks, and
            bought the drinks.
The moment was so contraband, it gave unto that liquor bar,
    A zest, he asked the constable to take another neat,
But lifting out his ticker, says the bobbie, " Well be quick
    or 'gar !
        The sergeant might come whop on me ! he's out upon
            his beat."
The constable decanted it, said he, " Howld on until I look,
        Now fly ! " said he, and while they dived again into
            the night,
He fished from out his overcoat, and deftly in his mouth he stuck,
        A friendly lump of orris root, to make his breath all right.
That bobbie was a wily one, the act was rather opportune,
        For they had scarcely managed to get half-way up the gut
When he was made aware that he must coin a whited
    whopper soon,
        For hark ! it was the tramping of the sergeant's heavy
            foot !
Said he, " We must dissimble, or I'm ruined, and a shapable,
        Excuse I'll have to make ! "   ⁕   ⁕   ⁕
            " What brings the two of you down here ? "
" I'm makin' just a Pres'ner, Sir, he's dhrunk, an' he's incapable,"
        Exclaimed the bobbie, gripping Binks, just under
            Binks's ear !
'Twas somewhat ominous for Binks, though he protested not,
    he chewed

The cud of thought, until he saw that sergeant out of
    sight ;
He had not comprehended yet, the patronising turpitude
    Of bobbies, who will take a treat, " well now," said he,
        " good night,"
But spake that constable, said he, "good night is best for you,
    ye see,
    But it won't answer now for me, I darn't let you go,
It's quietly, and aisily, and dacently, you'll come wid me,
    Yer dhrunk, an' yer incapable ! I towld the sergeant so."
Fitz-Binks fell plump in mire of doubt, 'twas shocking ! thus
    to realize,
    Such treachery, and subterfuge, of ingrate sneak of sin,
But 60 X was bigger in his figure, by a deal of size,
    And little Binks, was little, so the bobbie ran him in !
The sergeant,—he who took the charge—was grave, and staid,
    particular !
    He entered Binks upon his book, and sent him to the
        cell,
And Binks did forfeit half a sov., for standing perpendicular,
    Before the Beak, and leaving court, he cursed that
        bobbie well !
He said the act was scandalous, and of the gutter order, he,—
    That bobbie was, " Ah whisht ! ye see, an' howld yer
        tongue, shut up
It's fond of me, you ought to be, if I swore ye wor disordherly,
    It would have cost ye exthra, or you'd maybe be put up!"
It used to be a sermonising habit, and methodical,
    To tag a moral story, with a warning at its end
And bobbie entertainments in the midnight, might be quodical!
    So leave him to his duty, if you'd keep him as a friend.

A FUGITIVE KISS.

WAS on the carpet kneeling,
And fondly, and with feeling,
  I pressed her metacarpus,
      To my osculating lip,
    When flexor,
    And extensor,
  Of stern Parental censor,
  Incontinent did greet me,
      And took me near the hip !
I rolled into the fender,
With broken silk suspender,
    And motive movement sharp, as
        Her Pater gave the tip !
He didn't back the winner,
        For sport was not his grip.

The above brief but touching confession of disastrous failure, recorded by Timothy Pipkins,—a sporting student of St. Jago's Hospital,—is indicative of the Nemesis from an offended fate, that frequently foils the improvident hunter of matrimonial adventure.

THE BEDROOM CURSE

TIM DOOLIN was a well known jock,
    an active sprite, and light and trim,
And time there was, that jocks did funk, to mount, and run
    the race with him.
He won by length, he won by head, he saved the race by nose,
    and ear,
Till all the jocks, around their pints, exclaimed the thing was
    devilish queer.

AND THE

But fortune is a gay coquette ; by fickle fortune, Doolin lost,
Till every one who backed him, soon did find him out a fraud
    and frost.
I've seen him lose at Punchestown, I've seen him last, at
    Baldoyle too,
At Fairyhouse I've seen him fall—his colours then were black
    and blue.

MURDERED

He stood and scratched his head amain, beside the stable
    door one night;   ·
He had been drinking tints of malt, and felt as he were almost
    tight.
A race was on to run next day; he totted up his chance to
    win,
When turning thro' the stable-door, he saw a gentleman
    within !

He thought the thing extremely strange, and asked the man,
    why he was there,
And stoutly gave the hint, that he was there, to sneak, and
    dose the mare.
The gentleman, he laughed a laugh. " I've backed the beast
    myself, by gum !
And you must win, or I will be the loser of a tidy sum."

" Well, look," said Doolin, " pon me sowl, I have me doubts
    that she's in form."
The stranger glared at Doolin, and with voice, as of a rising
    storm,
Accused the jock of practices, that were not meet for honest
    men,
And asked him how he won so oft, and could not pass the
    post again ?
" Well, yis, yer honor, 'pon me faith, it puzzles me the same
    as you,
That I can't jerk the horse ahead, and win as once I used
    to do.
I never drink before the race.   I always pray before I mount:
And yet I find it's all the same ; my prayers have come to no
    account !"

" I used to curse and swear, but, ah, bedad, my swearing
    days are done ! "
" Then how on earth could you expect to be the man who
    could get on ? "
" I may not dare to curse and swear.   I have a rich, religious
    aunt,
I'm in her will, and I would lose the fortune if I did, and
    shan't.
She often heard me curse and swear; but warning me one
    day, says she :
If you go on to curse and swear, I'll have no more to do with
    thee !
I've made my will, and left you all my worldly goods, and
    money, too ;
I've got it written, signed and sealed, so you be careful what
    you do !'
I promised her, upon my oath, that I would neither curse
    nor swear,
And I have kept my word, and I will keep my word to her, so
    there !
She lent to me a cockatoo, and cautioned me, I must not lack,
To treat him well ; he's in the room I occupy, till she comes
    back."

" Ah, that, indeed.   Well, here's a tip : when in the morning
    you get up,
Keep cursing all the time you dress, and swear at night,
    before you sup,
By this no human ear will catch the oathings that will make
    you light,

And take a load from off your mind, and you will win the
   race—good night."

That very night when he went home, he slyly locked the bedroom door,
And up and down around the room he scattered curses, and
   he swore,
He cursed before, he cursed behind, he cursed until his face
   was red,
By dint of cursing, and at last he stripped, and tumbled into
   bed.
Next morning many oaths he made, and sandwiched them
   with many a curse,
That sounded weird, and wry, and strange; his oathings
   they could not possibly be worse.
He cursed because he had to rise, he cursed to leave the bed
   so nice,
And warm, and soft, he cursed because the water was as cold
   as ice.
He cursed around the basin-stand, he cursed the water jug,
   alas !
The towel and the soap he cursed, with oath that almost
   broke the glass.
He cursed a button that was loose, he cursed the thread and
   needle, new,
He cursed the irritating starch, he cursed his washerwoman,
   too.
He cursed his braces—they were tied with bits of string, that
   broke in twain,
He fixed them with a pin ; it stuck into his spine—he cursed
   again :

He cursed the postman for his knock—'twas by his tailor he
    was sent ;

He cursed the landlady who brought the bill ; and asked him
    for the rent.

Before, behind, above, below, at right or left, he was not
    loath

To drop a detonating curse, or fling an alternating oath.

He cursed the razor and the strop, he cursed the wart upon
    his nose,

He cursed his hair that wouldn't grow, he cursed the corns
    upon his toes.

He cursed a stud and button-hole that was too big ; and in the
    street,

He saw a burly constable, and cursed the man upon his beat,

He cursed the helmet on his head, the number on his collar,
    too ;

He cursed the stripe upon his arm, his mittens, and his suit
    of blue.

He cursed his baton right and left, he cursed it also upside
    down,

He cursed him to the county gaol and back again, and into
    town.

He cursed the lining of his sleeve, a bottle in his pocket—who

Had put it there he could not tell—he cursed his aunt, her
    cockatoo

He cursed the laces of his boots, the cockatoo he cursed again,

Again he swore, unlocked the door, and gaily started for the
    train.

Hurrah ! he won the race that day, and everything for him
    went right,

And surreptitiously he cursed and swore, and cursed again
     that night.

A painful shocking thing, that men should stoop to acts like
     this, for fame or pelf.
Thro' all my friends there's not a man would act so shocking
     but himself.
His calender grew bright again with fortune's sunlight o'er
     it cast,
But there must be an end to such, and retribution comes at
     last.
His aunt returned to town again ; he gave her back her
     cockatoo,
'Twere better he had slain him first ; it's what, I think, and
     so will you.
One day a mortuary note did come—alas ! his aunt was dead !
He buried her with decent haste, and then her latest will was
     read.
But by that testament, he found that he had not been left
     her purse,
It intimated this, that he had taught her cockatoo to curse !
It intimated this, that she thro' that, had met her death, alas ;
And in a codicil expressed a wish they'd send the bird to grass.

No mortal eye but his, beheld the deed he then essayed to do—
'Twas murder ! for he wrung the neck of his dead aunt, her
     cockatoo,
No mortal eye beheld the deed ; but things again with him
     went queer,
Till one day looking down the street, he saw a stranger
     prowling near.

The man who told him thus to swear, 'twas on a dark
    November eve,
He knew that stranger held a secret stone for him inside his
    sleeve ;
He knew that he had run a score of heavy debt, was due
    for sin,
And darting back, he closed the door. Said he to Bridget
    " I'm not in.
Just say that I am out," said he, and quickly up the stairs
    he flew,
The stranger knocked. " Ah, let me see," and up the stairs
    he mounted, too.
The servant sneaked the key-hole then, and saw a struggle
    on the bed,
Then ran below—" Mavrone, asthore, come up, agrah, the
    lodger's dead ! "

    *   *   *   *   *   *   *

The moral is of gentlemen you do not know, you should beware :
You should not use your bedroom, for a hiding-place, to curse,
    and swear.
To curse a harmless constable upon his beat, is even worse ;
'Twas he who caught the jurymen, who gave the verdict on
    his corse.
That shocking room is haunted now ; it may not raise a
    shock in you,
But every dark November eve, there comes a shrouded
    cockatoo,
And gliding in his pallid shirt, a wretched spectre doth rehearse,
The record of his oathings dire ! the cockatoo then shrieks
    a curse !

The man of easy habits then will see the deadly deed anew,
Of how the neck was wrung by him, who slew his aunt, her
    cockatoo.
The man of easy habits then, will see the evil sprite of gloom,
Come prowling for his guilty soul, and bear it down the trap
    of doom.

The landlady can never make the lodgers in that room content,
They never stay, beyond the day that she has asked them for
    the rent,
But men are not so wicked now ; they will not swear an oath
    for pelf.
They're much about the same as you—almost exactly like
    myself.

A GUN SOLO.

BY a lonely dried up fountain,
In a purple Irish mountain,
    My talk was interesting,
    With a female of that spot,
When she sprang from off my knees;
For rasping thro' the trees,
    A bullet stopped our jesting,
    I started at the shot !

" It's my husband's gun!"

        she murmured,

I sauntered from the spot !!

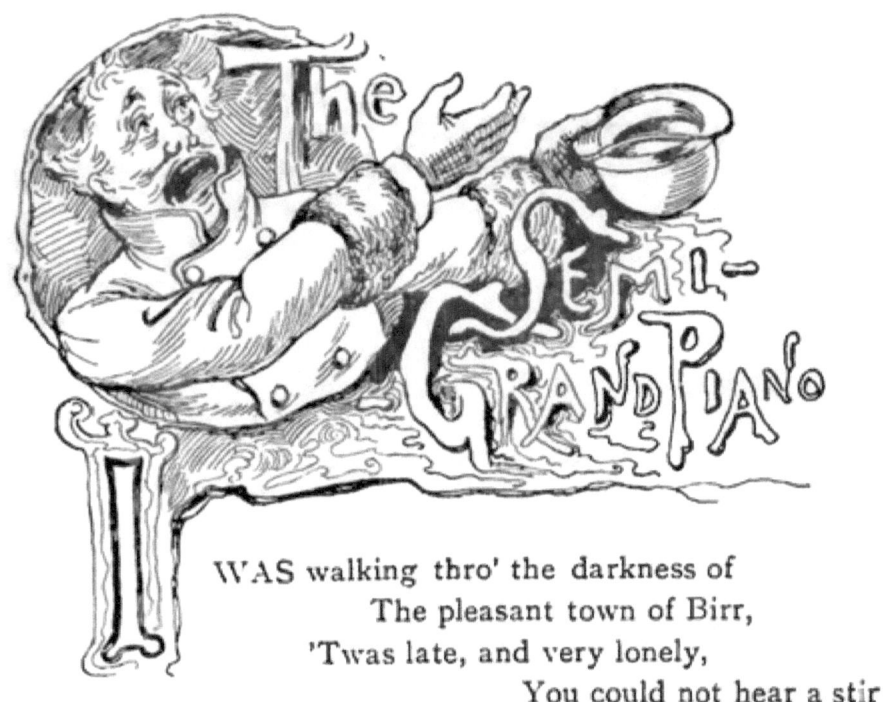

The Semi-Grand Piano

I WAS walking thro' the darkness of
     The pleasant town of Birr,
    'Twas late, and very lonely,
        You could not hear a stir
When turning round a corner, I heard the music sweet,
Of a semi-grand piano, and a singing down the street.

You will say it's not uncommon to hear the pleasant sound,
Of a semi-grand piano upon a midnight round,
But O the silver music, of the voice that mingled there,
With the semi-grand piano, was wonderful, and rare !

I waited on in rapture, and harkened to the strain,
I paused until she finished, and commenced the song again,
And O the magic pathos, of her voice was such, I say'd
" I'll warble when she's finished, an Italian serenade."

And so anon I warbled a heart bewitching thrill,
All in the friendly darkness, beneath her window sill,
I thought it might remind her, of the troubadours of old,
Tho' 'twasn't too romantic, for the night was dev'lish cold!
It wasn't all Italian, but it was much the same,
It was a sweet impromptu, a song without a name,
And if it doesn't bore you, I'll sing you just a verse,
You'll say it might be better; but I think it might be worse.

    " O lady who was singing
       With happy semi-grand,
    A troubadour is waiting,
       He's asking for your hand,
    Carrissima!   Mia!   Agrah!
       From other lands I roam,
    Be ready with the trousseau,
       I'll come, and take you home!

    Recordar, how I love you,
       This lay of mine will tell,
    O willow! willow! wirrasthrue!
       Mavrone!   I love you well!
    L'ami l'amo l'amantibus
       Ri foldherando dum,
    Mein fraulein cushla bawn agrah!
       Get up your traps, and come! "

It wasn't all Italian, this song of mine you see,
It wasn't like a tarantelle; 'twasn't like a glee,
'Twas thought of on the spur, its thus that brightest songs
  are made,
I think that you'll agree with me, 'twas a compo serenade.

I felt the song was working, 'twas amorous, and new,
'Twas making an impression, a thing I always do,
As tho' the middle ages, were back again in Birr,
Hark! hark behind her lattice, at last I heard a stir!

O there's nothing like the feeling that passes through the
      mind
When you know a lovely lady is pulling up her blind,
And my heart was all a-flutter, in that lonely street of Birr,
When I heard the curtains rustle, with the sylphid hand of her.

I saw the window open, I saw a face to scarce!
I heard a voice that muttered " What are ye doin' there? "
And over me was emptied a full and flowing can!
Which made me hurry homewards, a wet and wiser man!

I sang my song that midnight, with voice of dulcet tone,
My dulcet voice next morning was like a bagpipe groan,
A blanket round my shoulders, my feet were in a pan,
Some doctor's stuff beside me, a sad and wiser man!

CANTICRANK.

IF you have æsthetic notions of the classic beauty rare,
    You would never for a moment say that Nature took the
      prize,
For the elegance of figure, or tint upon her hair,
    Of Mother Becca Canticrank, you wouldn't like her eyes ;
        Her nose you couldn't admirate,
        Her teeth are in a chippy state,
Her voice is like a corncrake, her manner like a knife ;
        A cutting way of dealing
        With sentimental feeling,
You wouldn't altogether care to choose her for a wife.
But ah ! she is the casket of a compensating excellence,
    The odour of a sanctity peculiarly her own,
        She knows she is, without a doubt,
        Intensely moral out and out,
And so she sits in judgment on a self-constructed throne.
        As Censor of corruptousness,
        Of Nature in voluptousness,
She rails in holy horror, with a Puritanic rage,
        That beauty's form is shocking,
        In semi-raiment mocking,
Her own upholstered scragginess in picture or on stage.
        Her loathing is the ballet ;
        For lo ! from court and alley,
The thousand Cinderellas are fairy clad and bright,
        A direr deed of sinning—
        By dint of beauty winning

Their bread, than by the needle, in the murky candlelight,
    O Mother Becca Canticrank,
    The ways of earth are very rank ;
But women live by beauty, intelligence, and toil,
    And toil is overcrowded, Mam,
    Intelligence is got by cram ;
And what's for lovely Sally of the garret, shall she spoil ?
    No ! pray for her, and set her,
    As toiler for the sweater,
Or freeze her in the winter, on your doorstep in the street,
    With penance to her bones,
    By whiting up the stones,
That you may moil her handiwork with smirch of dirty feet.
    Or pray for her, and crape her,
    As vestal to the draper,
To do the woful penance, of Canticranks to please ;
    Till worn out and weary,
    Unto her bedroom eyrie,
She staggers up at midnight, then bring her to her knees;
    Do anything, but let her
    Enjoy a way, to better
The miserable midnight of her life, into the day
    Of brighter fortune's light ;
    Aye, crush her back to night,
And teach her how to thank you, by kneeling down to pray.
    Yes, hound away the ballet,
    Destroy the chance of Sally,
For she has many prizes in the marriage market won.
    By hypocritic prudity,
    Go boom the semi-nudity,
Of drawing room and salon, for the first and second son.

CAUGHT IN THE BREACH.

O^F fascinating parts,
    He played with female hearts;
        'Twas reprehensible, as you may guess;
But still it was his way,
Continued he to play,
        Until a maiden asked him for redress,
And folly bore the fruit,
Of breach of promise suit,
        He owns a couple of thousand pounds the less,
        He's a sorry man to-day, he does confess,
        And the wily way of woman he does bless,
        And his pipe is all that he will now caress,
        He doesn't care to think of it, the mess !

A KLEPTOMANIAC'S

DOOM.

THE Lord of Masherdudom wore on his essencèd curls
    A golden zone of strawberry leaves, and rays with pips of
        pearls,
Tho' he was called an Englishman his blood was Prussian blue,
Which unto his complexion gave a gallimaufry hue,
The Earl of Masherdudom, he was just as he began,
He seemed in perpetuity, a fossil ladies' man,
And yet he wasn't what you'd call an absolute success,
He hankered to be more, than most; he wasn't, he was less,
For he was poisoned with the grip of miser hungered greed,
And racking rent upon the screw, he made his tenants bleed.

He loved his Parson; for he taught that gold was dross, and
    scutch,
To men who of the sinful chink, had not got overmuch;
He taught by unctious homily, how really false, the leaven
Of gold is to a tenant here, compared with gold in Heaven;
But man with base ingratitude is rife, they did not bless
The Earl of Masherdudom, so he wasn't a success.

One day 'twas ruminating thus, alone, and in his club,
" My politics do fail " he said " to fail, aye there's the rub,
I was a high conservative; I am, what am I now?
An India rubber ball of wind, a pinhole in my brow,
Evaporated of my brain, a shrunken rag, and dust,
A something must be done I wot, I wis a something must; "
He took a portly bottle up, and from its tinselled neck,
He poured the buzzing nectar forth, and without pause or reck,
Into his æsophagus then decanting it straightway
He lit a weed,—he was a man who never smoked a clay,—

"Oddsbodkins to that liberal!"—
He swore in antient guise
Of quaintly oath—"He's more than I,
I wot, for he is wise
Unto the leading, and the light
That gives to men a glim
Of what they know is just, I'm but
A farthing dip to him,"

Twas thro' his indignation he did make a vulgar slip
And coined so rude a simile,—in re the farthing dip;
" I find my brains have broken loose, my occiputs to let,
But ha! I've got a last resource, that none may wot of yet,
I'll take my diamond ring to-night, and use it round his panes,
And in a mask I'll burgle him, and steal his liberal brains! "

He quaffed the glorious fizz again, a swill both deep and strong
Nor witted he, nor wotted he, it was a lawless wrong
To steal another's brains.   He then invested in some crape,
And putty, thus to make his nose more liberal of shape;
He turned his coat, its lining was of party colored trim,
And got a life preserver " now I'll go and burgle him! "

That night
He sneaked the toepath o'er,
    With serpentine device,
And round a postal pillar red,
    He scouted slyly twice,
Until on india rubber soles,
At length he reached the goal,
    And up the garden wall
        He clomb,
And down the wall he stole!

Then knotting on his mask of crape, with spry ambition fain,
He slid, and worked his diamond ring around the window pane,
He crept into the servant's hall, no maid, or cook was there;
He took his boots, and gaiters off, and climbed along the stair;
He sought to catch the banister, to guide his pilot fist;
But headlong down the flight he fell, the banister he missed!

And lo! from every room above, the shrieks of horror rose,
From girls in papered tresses, bereft of daylight clothes,
And full for twenty minutes by the clock, their cries increase,
Of "ho! Police" and "robbers hi!" and "murder ho Police!"
The butler fired a pistol shot, the cook discharged a spit!
The boots let fly a bootjack, and the footman all his kit!
The groom ran down the stable stairs with horsey oathings dire,
And a constable came knocking said he "are you's on fire?"

He put his bull's eye on him "Ha! well here's a putty case!
You needn't hide, behind that putty nose upon your face;
I'm on the 'wanted' tack for you a couple of months or three
So don't you be disorderly, move on, and come with me,"

They put him on his country, and the evidence was queer,
But said his Lordship solemnly,

"The crime that we have here,
"Is rare in English jurisprud', a noble drinks, and goes
With mask of crape upon his eyes, and putty on his nose,
To burgle certain premises, but drink being in his head,
Mistook the house, attacked his own, and burgled it instead!
Now this is queer; but I have here, a very antient law,
And from its context, you will mark, I this deduction draw,
That should a man by suicide, attempt to sneak away,
" From curses that grow thick on him, we make the coward
        stay,
And if a man by putty nose, and mask, and diamond ring,
Do burgle his own home, It's just a similar sort of thing,

And so unto the upper house, for thy remaining years,
I sentence thee!" and with his wig, the judge mopped up his
        tears.

AN ILL WIND

BLEW HIM GOOD!

I WAS to the windward walking,
Of love and marriage talking,
    When, zephyr like a feather,
        Took my topper on its wing
And I hollo'd ! and I hollo'd !
While another fellow followed,
    It stopped, they came together,
        With his foot upon the thing !
Æsthetic oaths I uttered,
A threat for damage muttered,
    And my popping of the question,
        Had also lifted wing.

   *   *   *   *   *   *

She's wedded to another,
And now I cannot smother,
    My blessing on that zephyr,
        And that fugitive top hat,
For had I not been checked,
My happiness was wrecked,
    I wouldn't be so rosy
        To-day, and round and fat.

THE GHOST
OF
HIRAM SMIKE.

S HE was a dainty lady, with golden hair, and cream
    Of roses, her complexion, belike a charming dream.
Her eyes were sapphire lighted, her lips, with peachen bloom,
Paterre of pearls were framing, but in her heart a tomb;
For many loves lay buried, that cemet'ry below—
O fie on it for ladies, with love, to trifle so.
At last unto a stranger, her stony heart, did strike,
His wealth was most romantic, his name was Hiram Smike.

'Twas on her mother's sofa he looked at her, said he,
" I'm kinder sweet on you, love, will you accept of me ?
I've travelled half this orange, and never saw your likes;
I calculate you oughter join the wigwams of the Smikes."
His wealth was most romantic, she answered him with tact,
Said he, " I'm off to-morrow, my trunk is ready packed;
I must be off to 'Frisco, to see my corn is barned,
Don't marry in my absence, for if you do, I'm darned !
Now play some tune, that's proper, to show that you're engaged,
Expressive of your promise, and how your heart is caged;
Strike up some soothin ballad, to tell how you'll be true,
And I'll work in a chorus, of Yankee-doodle-do."

Her fairy fingers wandered, along the ivory keys,
Of her new rosewood cottage, like warble thro' the trees ;
She sang, that she'd be faithful, all in a soothing strain,
While he worked in a chorus—and then he crossed the main.

It was a level twelve months, a fortnight, and a day,
Since Hiram Smike departed, and yet he stayed away ;
But she did wait no longer, and they were back from church,
It was the wedding breakfast, she's left him in the lurch.

" A health unto the bridegroom," and up they rose to drink ;
When hark ! a cry was uttered that made the lady think ;
A voice of an old woman, employed upon that day,
To do some extra tending, " look here," said she, " I say,
I guess you do not know me because I've shaved my chin,
I'm dressed like an old woman, but I'm a man within ;
I'm Hiram Smike, your lover, who left the Yankee shore,
To come back here to wed you, I'm darned for evermore.
You've lifted me like thunder, but you shall never boast
Of how you jilted Hiram—I'm off to make a ghost ! "
He said, tucked up his flounces, and, fluttering through the
        door,
He left them all astounded, and he was seen no more.
Next morning in the Dodder, upon the city side,
A man beheld a woman, come floating down the tide.
And far away in London, a bride, and bridegroom fled
From their hotel at midnight—a ghost was round the bed !

They sought a second lodging, but in the room, as host,
Was waiting to receive them that sad, intruding ghost.

They tried a cabman's shelter, but it was all in vain,
That tantalizing spectre was by their sides again.

Aye, even in the daylight, in Rotten Row, aloud
They heard an awful murmur like water thro' the crowd;
A moan as from neuralgia did on each tympan strike,
" His ghost is on the war path avenging Hiram Smike."

They tried the penny steam-boats, the railway underground,
The busses and the tramcars, but still they always found
That busy ghost around them, their lives could not be worse.
"O thunder ! " shrieked the bridegroom, " I'll seek for a
        divorce."

But when the court was opened, the judge refused to sit,
For every pleading lawyer had got a sneezing fit ;
And then there came the earthquake, the ruddy sunsets came,
When lo! quite unexpected, one night, they saw a flame.

A flash like a vesuvian, did by the table strike,
With a Satanic whisper, " You're wanted, Hiram Smike."
And from that curious moment, there is no more to tell,
They're having every comfort, I hear they're doing well.

WHY

DID YE DIE?

"O PAT, the blush is on your face,
　　　You're white, an' cowld an' still,
I'm all alone, an' by your side,
　　　Upon the bleak damp hill.
The beatin' from your heart is gone!
　　　The starlight from your eye,
Mavrone Asthore, O Pat agra!
　　　Arrah! why did ye die?

A sthrake of blood is on your breast,
　　　An' blood is on your brow,
O let me die meself, an' rest,
　　　It's all I care for now.
I want to go where you are gone,
　　　An' in your grave to lie!
Ah! Pat avrone, I'm all alone,
　　　Arrah! why did ye die?

Me curse is on the men avick !
            That brought you out this night,
That took you off an' made me sick,
            An' coaxed ye to the fight,
O sure 'twas wrong to give your life,
            An' lave your wife to cry,
Ah ! Pat you should have stayed at home,
            Arrah ! why did ye die ?

You wouldn't take me warnin', Pat,
            An' shun the moonlight boys,"—
" Ah ! Biddy whisht ! wake out of that,
            You're dhramin' ! stop yer noise !
Ye've dhragged the blankets off of me,
            I'm jammed against the wall,
An' you're bawlin' all for nothin' for
            I'm not dead at all ! "

A PRETTY LITTLE LAND I KNOW

A PRETTY little land I know,
  Surrounded by the pearly spray ;
It's where the em'rald shamrocks grow
      In fertile propagation.
The great bear in the polar sky
  Can see it at the fall of day,
When peeping with his glistening eye,
      Towards Britain's mighty nation.

For when the sun is rolling down
  Into the ocean for the night,
In all his radiant golden crown,
      And purple-flecker'd rays ;

R

While tucking on his dreaming cap,
  Inside the crimson curtains bright,
The great warm-hearted kingly chap,
        Looks back with loving gaze.

And where the shining waters dance
  Across the wild Atlantic deeps,
He takes a sudden, pleasing glance;
        And when the twilight cometh grey
On other shores, with coaxing glow,
  He winks his eye before he sleeps,
Upon that charming land I know,
        That's jewel'd in the pearly spray.

There, lore of bravest deeds enshrine
  Great phantoms of historic days;
There, myrtle wreaths of memory twine
        O'er many storied graves;
There, many marble brows are bound
  By sculpture of the poet's bays,
The while their souls are still in sound
        From harp strings to the waves.

With glorious wealth of hair in curls,
  And beauty, real elating, boys,
It's there you'll find most darling girls
        In plentiful diffusion.
And Cupid, with his bow and darts,
  His murders perpetrating, boys,
Don't care at all what crowds of hearts
        He slays by love's delusion.

HOW THEY ENLIST

TWO guardsmen, and a Dublin boy
      Were drinking in a bar
The Dublin boy was standing treat,
      Unto the men of War,
And thus to one, he speaketh so—
      The taller of the two—
" I wonder how men come to go
      And list, now how did you ? "

The soldier grinned a stately grin,
      In military style,
He meant it for the Dublin boy
      As patronising smile !
" It kind of sort like worries me,—
      This was the cause of that,
I always liked to feed on lean,
      I couldn't bolt the fat !

" One day, it was at dinner, see,
　　　　A big disgustin' lump
Of fat, was dumped upon my plate,
　　　　I got the bloomin' hump !
I merely took the thing upon
　　　　My fork, and with a sigh,
I let my father have the fat
　　　　Whop in his bloomin' eye !

" A sign of partnership dissolved
　　　　Between my boss, and me,
I took the shillin', and became
　　　　A guardsman, as you see,
But there ! my appetite has been
　　　　Most tricky like, and mean,
Now I can eat a pound of fat,
　　　　And I detest the lean ! "

THE KINDER-

—GARTEN WAY.

N a perfumed orange grove, a—
    —jacent to Cordova,
I taught the English Grammar unto a lady gay;
    The verb " to osculate "
    I taught to conjugate,
Corporeally depicted, in kindergarten way.
        But by eavesdropping trick,
        A caballero quick,
    With lapse of condescension,—
    But where I may not mention,—
        In dexter handed flick,
        The Spanish verb to " stick "
Corporeally inflicted, in kindergarten way.
    The verb " to do," he did it,
    For Spanish laws forbid it ;
        To translate free,
        Corporeallee,
    The verb " to love," and practice it,
    Upon the pupil, 'tis unfit,

> To illustrate,
> Its active state,
> When passive hate.
> Behind a gate,
> Doth lie in wait,

To teach the verb " to suffer,"

> In kindergarten way ;

He taught the verb " to suffer,"

> By impromt sword display,

I learnt the verb " to suffer ! "

> And would not, could not stay,
> So left upon that day,
> My fee he did not pay,
> His ingrate, Spanish way !

OPINIONS OF THE PRESS

ON

THE BARNEY BRADEY BROCHURES

BY

WM. THEODORE PARKES.

" It is pleasant to turn from these gloomy details to the hearty, rollicking, honest, joyous spirit of Barney Bradey. He sings the Prince's Installation to the tune to which *Ingoldsby* sang the Queen's Coronation, and with very much of the same spirit and success. The details are full of real good humour, and are thus picturesquely concluded with a touch of the Ulster King at Arms. Barney Bradey's eye was pretty well everywhere but it failed to see one incident of the day. . . . . All this is worthy of being sung by such a bard as the author of ' St. Patrick's Ruction.'"—*Athenæum.*

"Most people know Barney Bradey, and the more you know of him the better you like him. Perhaps very few of your comic poets have achieved such legitimate success as Barney, whether in ' St. Patrick's Ruction ' or, the ' Queer Papers,' or even in the fugitive pieces which come to us from time to time. The whole story of Napoleon's war is told in verse, with a genuine Irish humour, abounding in good points and suggestive images. The fun is quite of an original kind, and is really *sui generis.* The author has great command of language, expressive yet simple, and manages meter with uncommon skill. The strange inversions, provoking hyberbole, and quaint terms characteristic of Irish humour, are here lavishly displayed ; and the man who would not laugh with Barney, while yet appreciating his satirical truth, must be unhappy indeed. The range of thought, though extensive, is very germane, and the humourist discovers a tinge of that Byronic happiness in soaring high and still keeping the game in sight. We regret that we cannot quote a stanza or two from 'The Christening Cake' to prove to our readers that our praise is as well deserved as it is genuine."—*Freeman's Journal.*

" This is a humourous extravaganza, by the author of ' St. Patrick's Ruction ' and other comic rhymes, and is characterized by the same cleverness and quaint drollery. The ' baptism of fire,' the proclamations, letters, telegrams, projects, and incidents of the war, are represented in fantastic forms of illustration. The effect is as ridiculous as the author intends it to be."—*Daily Express.*

" Welcome Barney !—In many a quaint, merry, and most grotesque "fytte," our rollicking Irish Rabelais runs over the most marked opening incidents of the Franco-Prussian war. All the outlandishness of diction ; the funniness of Hibernian phonetic spelling ; the strange, wild, yet always true, similes and comparisons ; the madcap, boisterous, merry-making that characterized ' St. Patrick's Ruction,' and the ' Queer Papers,' are repeated, equalled, aye, surpassed in the CHRISTENING CAKE. Barney's history of the war ends at Saarbruck. We long to hear him on Weissembourg, Sedan, Strasbourg, Metz, and Paris. We lately noticed ' St. Patrick's Ruction,' a work as full of real Irish witticisms as any we ever perused, and one that has won its author unstinted praise. The orthography of the present brochure is as comically outrageous, the similes and comparisons as far-fetched, and yet as true to nature—the whole dainty tome as full of genuine, rollicking, open-hearted Irish fun and humour as ' The Installation ' or ' Sods from Puncherstown.' It is pathetic, comical--true to nature, true to art."—*Tyrone Constitution.*

" It is seldom in these days that one comes upon anything thoroughly and undeniably Irish in the matter of witty writing. But the productions of ' Barney Bradey ' are a refreshing exception to this doleful rule. In ' St. Patrick's Ruction,' and the ' Queer Papers,' we rejoiced to find that an original had arisen among us ; and now, in another production, we are pleased to see our first opinion verified. The design of the piece lies in the combination of fifteen poems in one ' harmonious whole.' The story ends with the capture of Saarbruck, and all throughout runs a vein of most pungent and telling satire."—*Post.*

"The clever author of 'St. Patrick's Ruction has presented the public with another exceedingly witty pamphlet. The language is well chosen, and is sure heartily to amuse the reader; there is a vein of well-directed satire in every line that exhibits the thoughtfulness of the apparent careless writer."—*Limerick Chronicle*.

"Barney sings in Anglo-Irish doggrel of the most exquisite and original kind. His readers, whose name is legion, will find him quite as entertaining in those 'Queer Papers' as when his comet-like genius first blazed upon the world in 'St. Patrick's Ruction."—*Limerick Reporter*.

"Barney Bradey is a poet of no ordinary powers. It is not going too far to say that he has acquitted himself to his own satisfaction, and also to that of others. His orthography is peculiar, and his fun and wit are thoroughly Irish. The droll and clever Barney is a queer character, but he is so full of humour and says so many witty things that he must become a favourite with every one."—*Dundalk Democrat*.

"This poem under notice is merry in the extreme, and displays an accurate knowledge of Irish character, and of the peculiar English in which it likes to display itself. The author wishes everybody to be agreeable, and sets a good example himself. Here is a description of the ladies present at the installation service, full of the gentlest satire. . . . In addition, there is prose, entitled 'Sods from the Turf of Puncherstown.' It makes merry, but most good-humouredly, with everybody and everything, and by many readers will be regarded as fully equal to most of Artemus Ward's attempts. We have not seen his 'Tails and Ballids,' but it is spoken of highly, and we do not think the present attempt is deserving of less praise."—*Portadown News*.

"This is a whimsical and clever little production, written in a style of orthography peculiarly its own, and conveying a vast amount of humour. The lines entitled 'O Law! there's a Star from the Sky,' are rich and full of humorous comicality, greatly heightened by their droll versification."—*Derry Journal*.

"The grand processions, crushing, crowding, cheering, are all graphically detailed by the poetic 'Barney.' Altogether, a very pleasant hour may be spent in company with our facetious friend, 'Barney Bradey.'"—*Carlow Sentinel*.

"Barney Bradey has acquired considerable success in his treatment of Irish wit and character, partly in prose and partly in poetry: the latter runs on in a clear stream of merriment, while the former, with rollicking fun, possesses an undercurrent of light wit, and occasionally of caustic sarcasm. Taken as a whole the little book is exceedingly readable, and as a bold venture on a very delicate field of literature, may be looked on as a decided success."—*Herald*.

"Barney Bradey will cause a merry laugh to many by his piquant humour and droll conceits. They display at times an acuteness of observation and a pungency of wit which is heightened by the quaint mode of expression used."—*King's County Chronicle*.

"Over Barney Bradey's Papers every reader is sure to laugh. They are full of fun and jollity. The only fault is their brevity."—*Malvern News*.

"Barney Bradey is one gem of the Isle. He understands the 'boys,' and expresses their opinions in a very cute sensible way."—*Kirkcudbrightshire Advertiser*.

"Barney Bradey's Papers are so droll that we cannot do better than give our readers the one 'Matrimonial.'"—*Eastern Post*.

"Barney Bradey's Papers will afford considerable amusement.'—*Ayrshire Express*.

"Barney Bradey's Papers are full of genuine humour."—*Greenwich Gazette*.

"The facetious style has an excellent exponent in the person of Barney Bradey."—*Brighton Daily News*.

"Prose or verse come equally facile to his exceedingly humorous and racy pen."—*Ecclesiastical Gazette*.